Saving Sara

For Peggy:

Hope you enjoy!

H. A. Olsen

H. A. Olsen

ISBN: 1-4536-4852-6
ISBN-13: 9781453648520

dedication: *This novel is dedicated to my wife, Lesha, the love of my life and the mother of my three beautiful daughters, Angela, Katie, and Shannon.*

chapter 1

OKAY, I'LL ADMIT it—renting a car and driving from Atlanta to Charleston wasn't my brightest idea. After all, I could have charted a jet and made the trip in no time, saving myself the hassle of traveling on a busy interstate on one of the busiest days of the year—the Friday before the Fourth of July. But I thought a few hours on the road might be a good way to reconnect with my sixteen year-old daughter, Sara, whom I hadn't seen in weeks. So I rented a Jag, hit the open highway, and now found myself zipping along at the breakneck speed of twenty-five miles per hour, thanks to an accident on the *opposite* side of the road that had everyone slowing down to gawk.

"This is ridiculous," I said to Sara as the car in front of me slammed on its brakes. "It's going take forever to get to the coast at this rate."

She glanced up from the IPod sitting on her lap. Tucking a strand of sun-bleached hair behind her ear, she asked, "Did you say something, Mom?"

I raised my voice another octave. "I said it's going to take forever to get to the coast."

Sara's forehead wrinkled. *"Ghost?* Why are you talking about ghosts?"

With a sigh, I reached over and plucked the earbud from her left ear. "There, maybe you'll be able to hear me better now."

Her mouth fell open. "Oh-my-God! I can't believe you just did that! I was listening to my favorite song!"

"Well, you're my favorite daughter, and I'd appreciate it if you'd turn that IPod off and have a conversation with me. You remember how that works, don't you? First I say something, then you say something. Then you say something, and I—"

"I know what a freakin' conversation is!" She jerked the earbud from her right ear and slumped low in her seat. "So what do you want to talk about?"

I ignored her less-than-enthusiastic attitude and said, "Well, why don't we start with the show last night. Did you have a good time? I'm glad your flight got in early so you could be there."

I was referring to the concert I gave at Philips Arena, the last stop on a whirlwind tour that took me to thirteen cities in four weeks. But that was all behind me now (thank God) and I was looking forward to spending a week alone with Sara at my seaside cottage on Folly Beach, a tiny barrier island just south of the Charleston Harbor.

"The concert was okay," Sara said with a shrug. "Until you did those country songs. I hate country, it sucks."

Her comment didn't surprise me—most things 'sucked' to Sara lately. Especially me.

"What's wrong with country?" I asked, knowing I was launching into a battle I couldn't win. "It's an awesome form of music. It lets you tell stories with your lyrics."

She shrugged. "Whatever. But I still think it sucks. Just like it sucks for you to take me hostage and make me go on this stupid vacation with you."

"So you think I'm taking you hostage, huh?" I said with a crooked grin. "Sure hope the cops don't catch me. I'd hate to get arrested for kidnapping."

She propped her bare feet on the dash. "It's not funny. And I don't understand why you wouldn't let me stay home in Malibu like I wanted to."

Here we go again, I thought, *like we haven't been over this a million times already.*

"Honey, you know Aunt Rita is going to Europe this week," I began, trying to hide my frustration over her refusal to drop the subject. "So that means no one would be there to supervise you. I wouldn't be a responsible parent if I let that happen."

"So in other words, you don't trust me," she shot back.

I gave her knee a pat. "Oh, baby, I *do* trust you. It's your boyfriend's raging hormones that I don't trust. Boy's his age—"

"So that's it!" she interrupted. "You think me and Alex are going to have sex, don't you?"

Although Sara and I had discussed the 'S' word many times in the past, I found myself blushing at her bluntness.

"I just don't want you to make a mistake that could ruin your life," I said. "I'm afraid if you were home alone it might be too tempting for Alex to come over and..."

"Seduce me?" She shook her head and rolled her eyes. "Really, Mom, don't you think I know how to say no? Besides, we've had plenty of opportunities to do it already, especially at his house. His dad is always going out and leaving us alone."

That got my attention. With a raised brow, I said, "Well, maybe I should stop you from going over there from now on."

She turned away from me. "Just forget it. You don't understand anything I try to tell you, so why should I bother?"

I tightened my grip on the steering wheel. "Sara, why do you always do this? Anytime I try to talk to you, you get all defensive. Now stop having a hissy fit and tell me what's going on with you and Alex."

She broke into laughter. "A hissy fit? What in the world is a hissy fit?"

"I'm a Southerner, and in the South we call what you just had a hissy fit. But never mind that, just tell me what's going on with you and Alex. You guys aren't getting serious, are you?"

"We're in love—if that's what you mean by getting serious."

I didn't know whether to laugh or cry, so I settled for a sigh. "Honey, you're only sixteen. Believe me, you haven't got a clue what real love is yet."

The icy glare she gave me was enough to frost the windows. "Maybe I know more about love than you do. At least I know how to hold on to a guy and keep him from slipping away—unlike *you*."

I pressed my lips firmly together, reminding myself that I had made a vow not to get into an argument with her—at least not today, anyway.

"That's really not fair," I said, straining to keep my voice even. "Your daddy's the one who cheated on our marriage, not me. I had no choice but to leave him."

Her response was quick and pointed: "Maybe if you had given him what he needed, he wouldn't have gone looking for it somewhere else."

Easy now, I told myself. *Don't let her get under your skin. You're taking her on this trip to patch things up with her, not make them worse.*

I silently counted to ten and said, "You know, that's not a very respectful thing to say to your mother. I think you ought to apologize to me."

She didn't say a word. Instead, she donned her earbuds and stared out the side window.

Why does this happen everytime I'm with her? I wondered as traffic began to move at a normal pace. As soon as the speedometer hit seventy, I clicked on the cruise control and—

BANG!

"Hey, what's going on?" I said as the steering wheel began to vibrate in my hands.

The road felt rougher and it became harder to steer.

"Something's wrong with the car," Sara said. Like I hadn't figured that out for myself.

"I think it's a flat," I said, and wrestled the car into the emergency lane. As we came to a stop, I recalled my ex-husband's reaction when I told him I was making this trip: "You're crazy to drive to Charleston without a bodyguard," he'd let me know. "You're a celebrity, for Christ's sake, there's always the possibility that someone could be stalking you. And what are you going to do if you break down or get a flat tire? Have you thought about that? Huh?"

"Have you thought about that?" I murmured under my breath sarcastically. God, I hated it when he was right about something.

Sara looked at me and frowned. "So what do we do now? Do you know how to change a tire?"

I turned off the ignition, folded my arms across the steering wheel, and rested my head on them. "If you think I'm getting out of this car and changing the tire, you're out of your mind. All we have to do is call the rental company and they'll send someone out to help us. I think the number is in the glove compartment."

Sara opened the glove compartment and peeked inside. "Is this it?" she asked, handing me a pink sheet of paper.

I nodded and reached into my purse for my cell phone. While I punched in the numbers, she asked, "Will it take long for them to get here?"

I attempted a reassuring smile. "Shouldn't take long, sweetie. This company is known for its quick response."

A friendly female voice on the other end of the phone asked if she could help me.

"Oh, hi," I said, "I've got a flat tire. Can I get someone to come out and fix it?"

"Certainly, ma'am," the woman said. "Can you tell me where you're located?"

I glanced at the panel-mounted GPS. "Um, I just crossed the border into South Carolina on I-20."

"Do you know what mile marker you're at?" she asked.

I looked at Sara and shrugged. "Sorry, I wasn't paying attention to that."

The woman didn't say anything. I waited patiently for her to speak again, but the phone remained silent. Finally, I said, "Hello? Are you still there? Hello?"

She didn't reply. One look at the phone's screen told me why—it was blank. Dead battery.

"Crap," I moaned. "What else is going to go wrong?"

"Great," Sara said. "Now what?"

"I have a power cord...except it's packed inside my suit-case. Guess I'll have to go rummage for it."

"Why don't you use my phone?" Sara said. She pretended to search the car for it. "Oh, wait, that's right—I don't *have* my phone because *someone* made me leave it home."

"And for a good reason," I reminded her.

"Yeah, Aunt Rita caught me smoking one lousy cigarette. Big deal."

"One cigarette leads to another," I pointed out. "Next thing you know, you're hooked."

She crossed her arms. "I just wanted to see what it's like. I think it's ridiculous for you to make me give up my phone for a month because of it."

"It's not open for discussion," I said as I pushed the button to unlock the door. "Now excuse me while I go find the cord." I was about to get out when I noticed a black SUV pulling in behind us. The driver, and only occupant, appeared to be male.

Sara looked over her shoulder. "Oh, shit, what if this is some kind of axe murderer?" she wondered out loud.

"You owe me a dollar, young lady," I said as I reached into the backseat for a pair of oversized sunglasses and a baseball cap. "Remember, I told you every curse word that comes out of your mouth is going to cost you. I'm not having my daughter talk that way."

"Whatever," she said, watching me pile my sandy-blonde hair into the hat. "You're really going to wear that? It makes you look so stupid. And everybody still recognizes you—especially the paparazzi."

"Well, let's hope this guy isn't the paparazzi," I said, slip-ping on the sunglasses. "Let's hope he's someone nice who wants to help us."

Sara looked at me like I'd just arrived from a galaxy far, far away.

"This is the South," I reminded her. "I know it's hard to believe, but nice people actually exist here."

"I don't care, I don't trust this dude," she insisted.

We both watched him emerge from the SUV. I thought he looked pretty safe, but Sara continued to worry.

"How do you know he's not some kind of freak?" she asked. "Maybe he likes to eat people, like that Hannibal dude in the movies."

The man walking toward us didn't strike me as being the cannibal type. Wearing a blue dress shirt and khaki pants, he looked more like a businessman in his thirties—a rather good-looking businessman at that, with wavy blonde hair and a trim, athletic build.

Judging him as being harmless, I lowered the window.

"Afternoon ladies," he said. "Looks like you could use a little help. Got a flat, huh?"

I nodded. "Thank you for stopping. But we're okay. I just need to find the power cord to my phone so I can call the rental company."

He stepped back and let out a long whistle. "*This* is a rental? Nice Jag! It's an FX model, isn't it?"

I shrugged. "I'm not really sure."

He smiled—the same kind of charming, boyish smile that made me fall for my ex-husband when I first met him.

"Well, I better get busy changing the tire so you ladies can be on your way," he said.

"Oh no, I don't expect you to do that," I told him. "I just need to get the power cord so I can call the—"

He held his hand up for me to stop. "Nonsense. It might take hours for someone to get here. I can have it done for you in a matter of minutes."

Despite my further protests, he convinced me to wait with Sara on a grassy knoll while he removed our luggage from the trunk, located the spare, and went to work changing the tire.

As I watched, I became increasingly concerned for my Good Samaritan's butt—quite literally, since mere inches separated it from the cars and eighteen-wheelers flying by. I didn't breathe easy again until he tightened the last lug and strolled over to the knoll to join us.

"That ought to do it," he said, rubbing his hands together. "Not quite the surgery I'm used to performing every day, but a successful operation never-the-less."

"You're a doctor?" I asked in surprise.

He nodded. "An orthopedist. You know, one of those guys who fixes broken bones and replaces knees and hips that have seen their better days."

"I'm impressed," I said. "I can't believe you took the time to help us."

"Well, my father taught me to lend a helping hand whenever I can." He chuckled and added, "Especially to damsels in distress."

He studied me for a moment. With his head cocked to one side, he asked, "Don't I know you from somewhere? You look awfully familiar to me."

"Oh, I hear that a lot," I said with a nervous laugh. "I guess I have one of those common faces."

He nodded, although I could tell he wasn't convinced. "Well, let me give you my card," he said, digging into one of the pockets of his khakis. "Just in case you ever need some orthopedic advice."

He handed me an engraved card that read *Andrew Langston, M.D.* I noticed the address—it was in the heart of Charleston's historic district, only a few miles from Folly Beach.

"Thanks, Dr. Langston," I said, tucking the card into the pocket of my shorts. "And thanks again for helping us."

"My pleasure. And please call me Dr. Drew. That's what all my patients call me." He paused and said, "I don't believe I got your name."

"It's Angela." I didn't mind telling him that because my fans knew me as A.J., a nickname my best friend gave me back in high school and later became my stage name. "And this is my daughter, Sara."

His eyes darted between the two of us. "*She's* your daughter?" he asked incredulously. "You look too young to be the mother of a teen."

It was more than just a compliment—it was the truth. I had Sara when I was only eighteen, much too young to be taking on the responsibility of raising a child, especially since I was unmarried at the time.

"Thanks," I said, "but sometimes I feel pretty old. Especially after I've been..." I almost said 'after I've been on tour' but stopped myself before it came blurting out. "Oh, gosh, look at the time," I said, faking a glance at my watch. "I really have to be going. Thanks again for helping us out. I really appreciate it."

I took Sara by the hand and led her to the car. I didn't mean to be rude to the doctor, but I was afraid the longer we stayed the greater the chance he might figure out who I was.

Once we were on our way, I stole a couple of admitting glances of Sara out the corner of my eyes. It was hard to believe how much she had grown lately, and how radiantly beautiful she had become. With her long blonde hair, bronzed skin, and sapphire eyes, she looked like Malibu Barbie incarnate. Beaming inwardly, I thought how she was the one thing I had done right in my life. I also couldn't help but remember all the people who had urged me to have an abortion when I discovered I was pregnant with her. But I didn't listen to them because I knew there was something special about the child I was carrying; that she would surpass anything I had accomplished and would take the world by storm one day.

"Why are you looking at me like that?" she asked, catching one of my glances.

I smiled. "No particular reason—except I'm proud of you. Anything wrong with that?"

She was quiet for a moment, then surprised me by saying, "Don't you think that doctor dude was kinda creepy?"

"*Creepy?* I didn't think he was creepy at all. I thought he was nice."

"I don't like him," she said. "And I didn't like the way he was checking you out. I saw him looking at your hand to see if you had a ring."

"I didn't notice him doing that," I said, wondering if it were really true. "Are you sure you're not imagining things?"

"No," she insisted. "I saw him. Just like I saw you checking out his butt when he was changing the tire."

I shot her an incredulous look. "I did no such thing! Your imagination is running away with you!"

"No, it's not. I saw what I saw. So did you think his butt was tight and cute?"

She said it in such a teasing manner that I burst out laughing. "Well, it wasn't bad if you want me to tell you the truth. But that doesn't mean I was staring at it."

This is great, I thought. *Things are finally lightening up between us. Maybe—just maybe—it's a sign of things to come and we'll have an enjoyable vacation together.*

It only took a few seconds for my bubble of elation to burst. It happened when Sara suddenly turned gloomy and said, "So maybe you should hook up with him so you can forget all about Daddy. That would make you really happy, wouldn't it?"

"Sara, I..."

She put her earbuds in and said, "Forget it. Just forget *everything.*"

Tears blurred my vision as I drove toward an ominous-looking thundercloud. I shivered as it reminded me of a storm that occurred long ago; one that had such a devastating impact on the barrier island we were headed for that it took years for it to recover.

But not me. I would never fully recover from that terrifying night when the world as I knew it came to an end. Yet here I was, returning to the very place where I came within inches of losing my life at the tender age of seventeen.

The place where the spirits of my family members waited to haunt me.

The place my dreams had warned me not to go to.

chapter 2

"ARRIVING AT YOUR *destination*," the GPS announced as I pulled into a driveway paved with crushed oyster shells. I turned the engine off and gazed at a simple two story house that stood on tall pilings.

"Here," Sara said, handing me a tissue. "I'm sure you're going to need this."

I took the tissue from her and gave her a smile. "You know me too well, don't you?" I said with tears pooling in my eyes. Some were happy tears, stirred by pleasant childhood memories. Others were sad tears, the result of an unspeakable wound that refused to heal.

"I don't understand why we come here if it makes you cry," Sara said. She unbuckled her seatbelt and added, "It's like you're going to a funeral or something."

"I'm sorry," I said, dabbing my eyes with the tissue, "but I can't help it. This is a very emotional place for me." I nodded toward the wooden stairs that led to the front door. "I remember the day I carried you up those steps for the first time. You were just two months old, such a tiny baby. I took you inside and went straight to a window so I could show you the ocean. You got the biggest grin on your face, like you were happy to see it."

Sara faked a yawn. "I've only heard this story a gazillion times. So you think we can get out this freakin' car now? I'm gonna die if I don't stretch my legs."

We were unloading our suitcases from the trunk when a familiar voice called out my name. I turned and saw Mrs. Turner, a robust woman with alpine-white hair who'd moved into the house next door ten years ago.

"It's so good to see the two of you," she cried as she rushed across the lawn to greet us. Although she was in her sixties, she had no trouble getting around. In fact, she could probably sprint faster than me.

"It's good to see you too," I said as we embraced. "Have you been doing okay?"

"Oh, honey, I've been surviving, that's about it." She released me and gave me a good looking over. "Lord, you sure are a sight for sore eyes, A.J. And you're just as beautiful as ever. You've even lost some weight, haven't you?"

I laughed. "A little. My personal trainer whipped me into shape for the concert tour."

"Well, you look like a teenager with that school girl figure of yours." Her eyes turned to Sara. "And speaking of a teenager, would you look at this lovely young lady? Lord, I know she's got to be turning some heads."

Sara beamed and thanked her.

"I bet you have to beat the guys off with a stick," Mrs. Turner said to me. "Has she got a boyfriend yet?"

"I do," Sara answered for me. "His name is Alex." She looked me square in the eye and added, "We're in love."

I narrowed my eyes at her and muttered, "Puppy love, how cute."

Mrs. Turner must have realized she'd opened up a can of worms, 'cause she quickly changed subjects by asking me what I thought of her house's new paint job.

I turned my attention to what used to be a white bungalow with black shutters. To my horror, it was now a flaming pink bungalow with teal shutters. And was that what I thought it was in the front yard?

No, it couldn't be, *could it?*

"You admiring the toilet?" Mrs. Turner asked me.

"I...I...I don't think I've ever seen one used as a birdbath before," I said.

She laughed. "I think it fits right in, painted pink and all, don't you think?"

I was speechless.

She laughed again. "Oh, hell, I decided to let my flamboyant personality shine through. If other people on the island don't like it, they can kiss my..." She looked at Sara. "Oops! Almost said a naughty word in front of my girl. Let's just say they can kiss my grits."

I remained speechless.

"Anyway," she went on to say, "I'll let it stay pink until it needs painting again. Then I'll get me some of that vinyl siding like you got on your house, A.J. I'm telling ya, I'm getting too old to take care of that old dump. And I can hardly afford the insurance and taxes on it, now that I'm on a fixed income."

I wondered how she was getting along now that her husband had passed away. She didn't have any children and her relatives never came to visit, so she lived a life that had to be terribly lonely. No wonder the poor woman was always so happy to see me and Sara. I guess we were the closest thing to a family that she had.

"So how long you gonna be staying?" Mrs. Turner asked me.

"A week," I said. "I'm looking forward to some R&R. That concert tour drained me."

"I seen you on TV the other day," she said with a grin that revealed crooked but white teeth. "That new song of yours sure is good. I like it that you're doing more country now."

"Country sucks," Sara butted in. "She's only doing it because she's too old to do pop."

I gave her the death stare. Mrs. Turner broke the tension by laughing and saying, "Well, you deserve some rest, honey, that's for sure. But just make sure you keep your eyes on Sara. Especially after what's been goin' on around here lately."

I cocked my head. "What do you mean, Mrs. Turner?"

"Ain't you heard?" she said, inching closer to me.

"Heard what?"

She looked around as if she were about to divulge a secret she didn't want anyone to hear but me. "It's just awful, honey," she began with a shake of her head. "We done had two teenage girls go missing out here in two weeks time. The police have been doin' all they can to find 'em, but so far there ain't been no trace of 'em. It's like they vanished off the face of the earth."

My hand flew to my mouth. "Oh, my Lord, that's awful! Were the girls from around here?"

"Both of them was vacationing with their parents, staying at rental houses. They went for a walk on the beach and never came back." She put her arm around Sara. "You make sure you keep an eye on our girl. I don't want nothin' like that to happen to her."

"I sure will," I said, vowing to myself that I wasn't going to let her out of my sight. "Thank you for telling me about this."

"That's what neighbors are for," Mrs. Turner said. "We're also good for inviting weary travelers over for a couple of beers after they get settled. So why don't you join me for a couple of cold ones on the porch after you unpack?"

"I just might take you up on that," I said with a grin.

Mrs. Turner gave me a hug, then ambled back to her yard. While she watered her banana trees, Sara and I struggled to tote our over-packed suitcases up the stairs to the front door. When we reached the landing, I took a moment to catch my breath.

"C'mon, Mom, it's freakin' hot out here. Let's go in," Sara said.

I nodded and unlocked the door.

As soon as it swung open, I heard the panicked cries of my parents and siblings.

"What's wrong, Mom?" Sara asked. "You look kinda weird."

I shook my head to clear the voices. "It's nothing," I said. "It's my imagination running wild with me."

I stepped inside, knowing I had just lied to my daughter.

chapter 3

IF YOU ASKED a real estate agent to describe my beach house, they'd probably come up with terms like quaint, cozy, and comfy. But we all know those are sugar-coated words that really mean cramped, tiny, and confined—attributes that Sara began complaining about right away.

"My bedroom closet at home is bigger than this whole place," she said as she set her suitcases down in the foyer. Wrinkling her nose in disgust, she added, "And it stinks in here! It smells muggy."

I couldn't help but laugh. "Sara, you mean it smells *musty*, don't you? Things can't smell muggy, honey. That doesn't make sense."

"Whatever. All I know is it stinks."

I placed my suitcases next to hers. "That's because the house has been closed up for a long time. The smell will go away as soon as we open the windows and let some fresh air in."

"What about the air conditioner? Why don't we turn it on instead?"

"Because I want to smell the salty air," I said as I walked across the creaky hardwood floor in the living room to the French doors that opened to the screen porch. "I miss it."

"We have salty air in Malibu," Sara said, following me. "So what's so special about the air here?"

I unlocked the French doors, swung them open, and drew in a deep breath. I smiled as my lungs filled with something that was more precious than oxygen. "It's Folly air," I told her with my eyes closed. "A mix of everything I love—sea spray, pluff mud, and freedom."

"If you ask me, it smells like rotting fish," Sara said. She followed me to a Pawley's Island Hammock suspended from the porch ceiling. I plopped into it ungracefully and stretched my legs.

Sara cast a disapproving glance at the beach. "The ocean is all the way up to the dunes," she observed. "There's nowhere to sit or lie on a blanket out there. And the water is gray and murky-looking. The waves suck too. How am I supposed to surf on waves that puny?"

I looked out at the Atlantic. "The beach always disappears at high tide because it's eroding away," I said with a sad sigh. "If they don't do something about it soon, houses like this one might get washed away."

It was a scary thought for me, but Sara had other ideas.

"I wish it *would* wash away," she said. "That way I'll never have to come back here again. Can't happen soon enough, if you ask me."

My first impulse was to scold her for being disrespectful. But then I reminded myself that yelling at her was not going to make things better between us. So I bit my tongue and said, "Honey, why don't you take your stuff upstairs and unpack? After you finish, we'll take a ride over to Bert's supermarket and get some groceries. Maybe we can check out the stores on Center Street and see if they have some beachwear that catches your eye."

She murmured a disinterested, "Whatever," and dragged herself inside.

I took advantage of the ensuing peace by closing my eyes and rocking in the hammock to the rhythm of the waves. In no time, the song of the sea worked its magic, loosening the knots in my shoulders from the long drive. It almost lulled me to sleep—that is, until I felt a tap on my shoulder.

I cracked an eyelid open. Sara stood over me with a look of disgust on her face.

"What now?" I asked.

"I hate this place," she said. "My bed is damp and yucky. There's no way I'm going to sleep in it like that."

I yawned, stretched, and turned on my side to face her. "Everything gets damp here, sweetie. It's the humid air."

"The shower upstairs is gross," she added. "It's got mold or something growing in it. I'm not going to use it until you do something about it."

"How terrible," I said with mocked concern.

"And the windows in my room are so dirty I can't see out them," she added.

I shook my head. "In a five star hotel like this? Who would have thought? I guess we should notify the management. Maybe they'll give us a night free."

She glared at me. "It's not funny. And I found a dead roach in my room. He's really big."

"We call them palmetto bugs in South Carolina, honey. Not roaches."

She narrowed her eyes. "It's a *roach*, Mom. One with wings." She flapped her arms to emphasize the point.

"But we prefer to call them palmetto bugs down here. It sounds nicer."

She stomped her foot. "I don't care what you call them! It's disgusting!"

"Well, at least he's dead—you should be thankful for that." I rolled onto my back and laced my hands behind my neck. "So, while you're on a roll, is there anything else you would like to complain about?"

"Yeah, I can't get the Internet on my laptop."

"That's because there's no Wi-Fi. Why would I pay for the Internet when we're hardly ever here?"

Her mouth opened wide. "*What?* You mean there's no way to get online?"

I nodded. "That's right. Don't you remember? There's no cable TV, either—just the local stations. When I come here I like to—"

"No cable? No Internet?" she interrupted. "Holy crap, this is like freakin' Isolation Island on *Survivor*! Why are you torturing me by making me stay here?"

"Because I want us to spend some time together without distractions. If you had the Internet, you'd be on it day and night, chatting with Alex. I want you to talk to *me* for a change. I want to—"

"I'm going to die without the Internet! What am I supposed to do with myself?"

I smiled slyly. "You really want something to do? Well, let me give you a few suggestions. First, you can clean that gross shower stall. Then you can take some Windex and clean the windows you can't see out of. After you finish that, you can wash the sheets on your bed so they don't feel damp and yucky. And if you're still bored after that, you can—"

"Forget it!" She turned and stormed off.

It couldn't have been more than ten minutes later when I heard her muffled voice cry out, "Mom! Come here quick!"

I got out of the hammock and rushed to the foot of the stairs that led up to her bedroom. "What is it?" I called out.

"There's no toilet paper!" she hollered back. "I didn't look before I had to poop. Do you have any in your bathroom downstairs?"

"That's why I always tell you to look before you leap," I said.

"Mom! Stop talking and get me some toilet paper!"

I'd had enough of her rotten attitude, so I decided to have some fun at her expense.

"I'm afraid we don't have any toilet paper," I hollered back. "I guess I'll have to get some when I go to the store."

"WHAT? You're kidding, right? Please tell me you're kidding!"

"Nope. Just sit tight and I'll run down to Bert's and get some. I'll be back in a few minutes."

"You can't expect me to sit on this stupid toilet while you go to the store! Can't you bring me some paper towels or something?"

It was hard not to laugh. "Afraid we don't have any paper towels, either."

"This sucks! I can't even get the stupid toilet to flush! I hate it here! I hate it more than anything! I want to go live with Daddy!"

"Sorry to hear that," I said like I didn't care. "I'll be back in about thirty minutes. If you want the toilet to flush, you need to turn the little knob at the bottom of it so the water flows again. You need anything else besides toilet paper?"

"MOM! Don't you *dare* leave me stranded on this commode!"

"I won't be gone long, honey. Maybe you can read something while you wait. You want me to bring you a magazine? Maybe you can tear out a couple of the pages and use them for toilet paper."

"That's it! I'm leaving! As soon as I get up I'm calling Daddy and ask him if I can stay with him—forever!"

I climbed the stairs, opened the hallway closet, and found a roll of Charmin. I took it to the bathroom and tossed it to her.

"Here," I said, "I was only teasing you, so stop having a hissy fit."

"I still hate it here!" she said as I walked away. "And I hate you for making me come here!"

For a moment, I felt my mother's presence. It was like she was standing beside me, whispering words of encouragement: "It'll be okay...just give her time...Sara still loves you. She's just upset over the divorce, that's all."

I shivered from a chill running down my spine and went downstairs to unpack.

chapter 4

THE NEXT AFTERNOON found me lying in a lounge chair by the edge of the sea. With my eyes closed, I basked in the sun while listening to the soothing sound of the surf and the haunting cries of the gulls. It was the most relaxed I had been in days.

Then the stupid tide rushed in.

It was like a mini-tsunami. In a matter of seconds, the sand that had been supporting my chair disappeared under the foamy rush of the Atlantic, causing it to collapse and spill me into the water.

"Sucks to be you, huh?" Sara called out. She was sitting cross-legged on a blanket near the dunes, laughing her butt off.

I grabbed my chair and took a quick look around to see how many people had witnessed my embarrassing tumble into the sea. Fortunately, it was a weekday and the beach was pretty deserted, except for a young mother who happened to be walking by with her five year-old son. The little boy pointed at me and said to his mom, "Look, that lady fall out of her chair and get wet! She didn't know the water was coming!"

I pretended like I didn't hear him and trudged up the sand to where Sara was.

"I've never seen the tide come up that fast," I told her as I unfolded my chair and flopped my soggy butt into it. "It must be a full moon or something."

"All I know is it was really funny," Sara said. "And I got the whole thing captured on my web cam."

"Your web cam?" I looked over and saw her laptop sitting beside her. "What are you doing with that out here?"

"Chatting with Alex. He said to tell you he's sorry you got wet."

I gave her a puzzled look. "Wait a minute, how are you getting online when we don't have WiFi?"

She grinned. "I found a signal I could tap into. I guess it's coming from one of the houses next to us."

"That's not a good thing to do," I said, lowering my chair a notch. "It's like stealing."

"That's ridiculous, Mom."

"No, it's not. They're paying for the service, not you. You have no right to use it without their permission."

"Okay, okay, enough with the lecture." She slid her sunglasses down her nose and squinted at me over the rims. "God, Mom, did you know you're burnt?"

I glanced at my legs. She was right; they were turning the color of boiled shrimp.

"Crap, I can't believe it," I moaned. "I used to tan so easily, but now all I do is burn."

"You're getting old," Sara said. "Your skin's not as good as it used to be."

"Thanks for reminding me," I said, frowning. "So I guess I better head inside before I get melanoma."

I was about to get up when I heard my cell phone ring. "I thought I left that inside," I said. "What's it doing out here?"

Sara reached under a towel for it. "Um, I sorta borrowed it," she said timidly.

I felt my blood pressure rise. "You *what*? I thought I told you no cell phones for a month. You're on restriction, remember?"

"I couldn't help it, Mom. I wanted to talk to Alex sooo bad. I really miss him."

"So you disobeyed me? Do you want another month of restriction? 'Cause that's what's going to happen if I catch you with it again."

"That's so lame," she said as she handed me the phone. "I'm getting too old for you to be punishing me like I'm some kid. I'm sixteen, Mom. I'm almost an adult."

"*Almost* is right," I said. "And until you *are* an adult you're playing by my rules."

"Well, I think it's ridiculous. All I did was try one stupid cigarette. It's not like I was smoking pot or snorting cocaine." She rose to her feet. "I don't know why you have to make a big deal out of everything. I wish you were more like Daddy. He never overreacts."

"That's because your daddy is just as irresponsible as you are. He's never going to grow up."

The phone continued to ring. I didn't care; I had more important matters to tend to, like winning this argument.

"You're always cutting Daddy down," Sara said, bending over to get the laptop.

My eyes nearly left their sockets. Peeking out from the top of her bikini bottoms was the tattoo of a butterfly.

I leapt to my feet. "Sara, what the hell is that?" I demanded.

She looked over her shoulder at me. "What the hell is *what*?"

I pointed to her butt "That...that thing!"

She grinned. "Oh, that. Isn't it awesome?"

"No, it's not awesome! And for your sake, you better tell me it's a phony!"

She turned to face me. "It's real. I got it when I stayed with Daddy last month. He has a friend who owns a tattoo parlor. I told him I was eighteen, and he was stupid enough to believe me. So I snuck down to the parlor one day and he did it for free. I think he was on drugs or something, but who cares? Isn't it beautiful?" She turned around and pulled her bottoms down lower to give me a better look.

"No, I don't think it's beautiful!" I cried. "And I want the name of the guy so I can have his ass arrested!"

"Chill out, will you? Daddy got all pissed off when he found out about it too. But then he calmed down and told me it was kinda cool."

"You're dad thought it was *cool?*" I threw my hands up in frustration. "He must be out of his freaking mind! And what were you thinking, Sara? Do you know what kind of message you're sending with that...that insect on your butt? God, what's wrong with you?"

"*You're* what's wrong with me!" She started for the house.

"Sara, stop!" I called after her. "I'm not finished yelling at you yet!"

She didn't slow down.

I collapsed into the lounge chair and covered my face with my hands. *A tattoo. How could this happen? Why didn't her dad watch her better? I ought to call him and give him a piece of my mind...*

The phone rang again.

I checked the caller ID. It was my best friend, Suzanne Richardson.

I brought the phone to my lips and said hello.

"About damn time you answered!" she yelled in my ear. "Why didn't you pick up the first time I called?"

"You don't want to know," I sighed. "It's bad."

"It's always bad with you. That's why I haven't called in a while. You're depressing as hell sometimes."

"Thanks a lot. But this is *really* bad. Sara got a tattoo."

"So? I've got one too. What's the big deal?"

I rolled my eyes. "The big deal is she's sixteen, Suzanne, not in her thirties like you."

"Damn, you had to bring up that thirty thing, didn't you? That's why I called—I need a shoulder to cry on. You know that asshole at Universal I was telling you about the other day?"

I knew where this was headed. Suzanne was one of the most sought-after actresses in Hollywood, but lately she'd been losing parts to younger women. Whenever it happened, she called me to vent. But I wasn't in the mood to console her—not after finding out about my daughter's tattooed backside.

"Are you listening to me?" Suzanne asked impatiently.

"Yeah," I said. "I'm sorry if I seem a little spacey, but I have a lot on my mind."

"Well, so do I. That S.O.B. at Universal had the nerve to tell me I was too *mature* for the role I wanted. You know what that *really* means, don't you?"

"Not really," I lied, although I knew exactly what it meant.

"It means he thinks I'm too old! Can you imagine that? Especially after all the money I've spent on enhancements. I think I look just as young as I did when I was in my twenties, don't you?"

"Well..."

"I even got a boob lift." I heard her slurp something through a straw. "You ought to see the girls now. Sitting high and perky. I'm really proud of them."

"Suzanne, what are you drinking?" I asked warily.

She didn't answer right away—a sure sign that she was thinking up a lie.

"It's a smoothie," she finally offered.

"Sorry, but I don't believe you," I said. "So come clean."

"Damn, you know me too well, don't you? Okay, it's a freakin' frozen margarita. It's a nice day and I'm sitting by the pool enjoying it."

"But you just went to rehab! Why do you want to—"

"Look, I didn't call to get lectured at," she butted in. "I called because I need a friend. But if you're going to start preaching at me, I'm gonna hang up."

"I can't help it if I care about you. I don't want anything to happen to you."

"Nothing's going to happen to me. But it would sure help if I could get away for a while. Maybe I ought to charter a jet and come down there. Wouldn't you and Sara like to have some company?"

"Well, I was sorta hoping to be alone with her," I said. "I think we need time together to—"

"I can get there in the morning," she continued, obviously not paying a bit of attention to what I was trying to tell her. "I think I'll start packing."

"But, Suzanne, you're not listening. I think Sara and I need time—"

"It'll be like old times. You, me, and the beach. I bet we'll have a blast."

"Suzanne, please listen. I came down here because—"

"Then it's a done deal. I'm calling the charter company right now and book a jet. God, this is going to be so much fun. You're still at the same house, right?"

"Right," I answered reluctantly.

"Cool. Make sure you go down to good ol' Bert's and pick me up some beer. I love to drink beer on the beach. But make sure it's lite—I don't want to put on any pounds."

"Suzanne, I'm not—"

"Okay, got to go. Love you, girl. Can't wait to see you and Sara. Ciao."

And just like that, my plans for a one-on-one vacation with my daughter crumbled like a sand castle at high tide, to be replaced by a reunion with an old friend whose constant companion was spelled T-R-O-U-B-L-E.

chapter 5

THERE WERE SOME things I wouldn't dream of doing in California. One of them was going to the grocery store. To do so would risk an encounter with the paparazzi or an overzealous fan, so I had grown accustom to letting my Aunt Rita, who lived with me in Malibu, do all the shopping for us. I had also grown accustom to her doing all the cooking, which was a good thing considering how inept I was in the kitchen.

But things were different here on Folly. I didn't have Aunt Rita to depend on, so unless I wanted to be responsible for my daughter starving to death, I was going to have to prepare a few meals. I figured even a kitchen klutz like me could throw a few sandwiches together and bake a frozen pizza or two. So I sat down at the dining room table and made a list of anyone-can-make-them meals. Then I tossed the list into my purse and took a little trip to Bert's.

No larger than a typical convenience store, Bert's is truly a Folly icon, a place where shoppers walk the aisles barefoot, wearing nothing but their bathing suits. It also serves as a hangout for the locals, which means gossip is fresh and cheap, like the eggs they sell. Open twenty-four hours a day, three hundred and sixty-five days a year, the quirky little store had earned its motto 'We may doze but we never close.'

Luckily for me, the store was nearly empty when I arrived. Not that I was worried about the locals spotting me—they were wonderful about respecting my privacy and keeping my stays on Folly a secret. But it was almost the Fourth of July, which meant the island was teaming with tourists. All it would take is for one of them to find out I was vacationing at the beach and I would have to spend the rest of the week looking over my shoulder, wondering if the paparazzi were lurking behind a sand dune, waiting to snap a picture of me or Sara in a bikini.

But today there were only two shoppers in the store besides me—a hippy-looking guy who looked strung out on drugs and a new mother in search of formula for her baby—so I was able to get in and out with everything on my list in short order.

There was one thing I didn't get, though: the beer Suzanne had asked me to pick up. I wasn't about to contribute to her drinking problem, so the only alcohol I purchased was a bottle of Arbor Mist for me (cheap stuff, I know, but Bert's wasn't exactly a place to shop if you were a wine connoisseur).

Anyway, it was twilight by the time I got back to the house. The sunset was so spectacular that I stayed in the car for a while to admire the deep pink and purple painted on the western sky. Then I began the arduous task of lugging the groceries up the stairs to the front door.

I was about to reach the landing when I heard something that made me stop cold.

It was the sound of an acoustic guitar, coming from the open window in Sara's room.

"I'll be darned," I whispered in awe as I set the bags down. "She's actually playing again."

Her voice wafted on the breeze as she sang the lyrics to 'The Cord That Binds,' a ballad I wrote many years ago after visiting St. Jude's hospital. It was a real tear jerker; a story set to song about a mother's love for her dying child. Why Sara picked it to sing now was beyond me.

I was also surprised that she'd found my old six-string. I'd hidden it away in the closet in my bedroom, just in case I got inspired to write a song during one of my stays at the beach. How she knew it was there was another mystery.

After she finished the song, I quietly opened the front door and slipped off my flip-flops. Then I placed the groceries on the counter, careful not to make a sound, and tippytoed toward the stairs.

I climbed them slowly, hoping they wouldn't creak and give me away. Just as I reached the last step, Sara began strumming the guitar and singing another song. This time it was something fresh from the charts—'Bad Day' by Daniel Powter.

She was starting the second verse when I gave the knob a twist and pushed the door open.

"Holy crap!" she shrieked when she saw me. "Why are you sneaking up on me?"

She jumped up from the bed where she'd been sitting and handed me the guitar.

"I heard beautiful music, so I wanted to check it out," I said. "You sounded really good—you haven't lost your style."

"I was bored to tears," she said, turning to face the window. "That's the only reason I was doing it. So don't think it means I'm going to start playing again. I hate the guitar and I hate singing."

"Could have fooled me," I said, setting the guitar down on her bed.

"Don't leave it there. Take it back downstairs with you."

"But you might want to play it later. So why don't you keep—"

"I don't want it!" she snapped. "Take it away!"

I put my hands on my hips. "Honey, I don't understand why you're acting this way. You used to love to play and sing. What made you want to stop?"

She didn't offer an answer.

"It's me, isn't it?" I said. "You're doing it to punish me for the divorce, aren't you?"

A breeze filtered in the window and lifted her hair from her shoulders. "No, I stopped because I hate to play music."

"I don't believe you. And you don't how sad it makes me for you to turn your back on your talent."

She turned to face me. With quivering lips and misty eyes, she said, "You think you know what sad is? Well, you don't know shit about being sad. Why don't you try my life for a while if you really want to know what sad is? Why don't you try having a mother and a father who are on the road more than they are home? Why don't you try living with one parent, then the other?" She burst into tears. "Why don't you try having your aunt raise you because your mother's too busy doing concerts and making CDs? Try that for a while and you'll see what sad is!"

I went to gather her in my arms, but she pulled away.

"No! Leave me alone!" she sobbed. "There's nothing you can do to make things better. You already ruined my life by divorcing Daddy!"

I started to cry too. "I'm so sorry, baby. I know how rough all this has been on you. But I swear I'm gonna make it better. Just wait and see."

"The only thing that will make it better is if you take Daddy back."

I shook my head. "I can't do that, Sara. Your dad cheated on me—more than once. Don't you understand that?"

She threw herself across the bed. "You always blame everything on him! But it's just as much your fault! All you ever worry about is your career. That's why he cheated on you—you were never around for him!"

"That's not true. Your daddy cheated on me because he never grew up, honey. He couldn't resist all the temptations that go with being a rock star—especially the women who throw themselves at him. How was I supposed to ignore that?"

Sara tossed her pillow across the room, almost knocking a picture off the wall. "Just go away! I don't want to talk to you anymore! Daddy's the only one who really understands me. I want to go live with him forever. I hate being with you!"

I sat on the edge of the bed and stroked her hair. "I know you don't mean that, baby. And no matter what you say, I'll always love you more than anything on earth."

"I don't care!" She shot up from the bed and ran out the door.

I followed her into the hallway. "Sara, stop. We really need to talk about this."

She bolted down the stairs.

I chased after her, but I was no match for her young legs. By the time I reached the living room, she was already out the French doors and on her way to the beach.

"Sara, I don't want you out there after dark!" I hollered from the screen porch. "You know what Mrs. Turner said about those missing girls!"

She ran to the edge of the sea, then turned and quickened her pace.

I cried out again for her to stop.

It was in vain.

A gathering sea mist swirled around her and wrapped her in a wispy shroud.

Then she was gone.

chapter 6

"NOW HONEY, I want you to stop fretting over that child," Aunt Rita said, her voice steady and reassuring on the other end of the phone. "Sara just needs to let off some steam. You used to do the same thing when you were a youngin'."

She was right; I couldn't remember how many times I had run out on the beach to escape my parents after they did something to piss me off. I even had a special place where I would sit and sulk—an old palmetto log that had washed ashore near the west end of the island. With my butt planted on the petrified log and my feet dug into the sand, I would pray for the day to come when I could break free of my parents' tyranny and be on my own.

Little did I know how quickly that day would come; how suddenly and violently it would occur. If it hadn't been for Aunt Rita, I would have probably found myself in a foster home or an orphanage. But she opened her home and her heart to me, and it didn't take long for me to fall in love with her simple, country ways. Although some would call her a redneck, I only saw a woman with an abundance of common sense and an uncanny knack for making your problems seem small. That's why she was the one I always turned to when I needed a shoulder to lean on.

"I'm just worried about Sara being on the beach after dark," I said as I opened the bottle of Arbor Mist I'd bought at Bert's. "My neighbor told me some girls have gone missing out here."

Aunt Rita laughed. "Honey, Sara can take care of herself just fine. She showed me some of that karate and jip-you stuff she's been learning, and let me tell you, she can kick some butt!"

I almost choked on my laughter. "*Jip-you* stuff? I think you mean jitsu, don't you?"

"Aw, I ain't no good with them Chinese words, you know that. But I'm just letting you know Sara can take care of herself just fine."

"I hope you're right," I said as I poured a glass of the Arbor Mist. "But I can't help but worry."

"That's 'cause a good momma always worries about her children. Your momma use to worry about you all the time too. She'd call me up and say stuff like, 'I don't know what I'm going to do about that Angela...all she does is stay in her room. It's like she's a hermit crab.'"

It was true—I did act like a hermit crab in my teens, preferring to stay inside my room and write songs rather than socialize. Sadly, my parents never knew about my budding talent. Back then I hid all the lyrics I wrote, thinking they were too personal to share with others. So I kept notebooks full of them locked inside in a wicker chest. A wicker chest that, like so many other things, was lost on the night that I became an orphan.

"Honey, are you listening to me?" Aunt Rita said, breaking me away from my thoughts.

"Sorry," I said, taking a sip of the wine. "Guess I zoned out for a moment."

"Are you sure you're okay? I know you must be drained after doing all those concerts. And I know the divorce must be weighing heavy on your mind. I hope you're not turning to alcohol to ease the pain."

"Just a little wine here and there," I said as I strolled out to the screen porch. "Just enough to take the edge off." I flopped into the hammock and added, "Don't worry, I'm not going to let myself become an alcoholic like Suzanne."

"I can't believe that girl invited herself to come down there," Aunt Rita scoffed. "Didn't you tell her you wanted to be alone with Sara?"

"I tried to. But you know Suzanne—she only hears what she wants to hear."

"You mark my words, she's gonna cause you trouble. There's screws holding my car together tighter than the ones holding her brain together. And have you seen what they said about her in *Star* magazine?"

"Aunt Rita, they've said some pretty nasty things about me too," I pointed out. "You can't take anything those trash magazines print seriously."

"They say she's doing cocaine," she said, obviously not swayed by my comment. "They say she's refusing to go to rehab. They predict she's gonna self-destruct and end up dead before the end of the year."

I rolled my eyes. "Yeah, and they said I was suffering from depression and was becoming bulimic. Guess they haven't seen me in a bikini lately."

"You *have* lost a lot of weight. But you look good, girl. You need to start using them looks to get another man in your life."

She was leading the conversation down a path I had no desire to travel, so I said, "I gotta go now. Been nice talking to you."

"You ain't gettin' rid of me that easy. Not until you stop moping over Randy and get you a new beau."

"I'm not moping over Randy; I'm glad I got rid of him."

"Fool yourself if you want, but you ain't fooling me."

"I don't want to talk about it."

"You *need* to talk about it. That's your problem—you keep everything locked inside you. You're gonna give yourself an ulcer like that."

"Oh, I think I see Sara coming," I lied. "Better go. I love you, Aunt Rita."

"You better not be fibbin' to me. You ain't so old that I can't tan that hide of yours!"

"I'm not fibbin'. Call me when you get to Paris, I want to hear all about your art classes. Love ya."

She sighed. "I love ya too. Even though I know durn well you're fibbin'."

I disconnected and closed my eyes. I didn't mean to rush her off, but I simply wasn't in the mood to talk about Randy. Anyway, it was over and done, so what was there to discuss? He did me wrong, I told him to go to hell, and that was that. End of story.

So why do you cry about it every night?

It was that damn pesky voice inside my head. I told it to shut up.

So why do you feel like there's a hole in your heart? the pesky voice asked, *and why do you look at those old photos of you and him and reminisce about the way things used to be?*

"Shut up or I'm going to drown you," I warned the voice. "A few more glasses of this wine and I bet you'll stop bothering me."

It didn't take long for my prophecy to come true. Two glasses was all it took to still the voice. Now I wanted to dance.

I wanted to dance because someone was having a party a couple of doors down and was playing the radio so loud that I could hear it clearly on the porch. My body yearned to move to the beat of Michael Jackson's 'Billie Jean' and AC/DC's 'You Shook Me All Night Long.' But the hammock was so darn comfortable that I settled for swinging back and forth in it.

After a while, nature called. On the way back to the porch from the bathroom I grabbed the bottle of Arbor Mist from the kitchen so I wouldn't have to get up everytime I wanted a refill. When I got back to the hammock I was happy to hear the sounds of Jimmy Buffet blaring from the party house.

I sang along to 'Margaretville' and 'Cheeseburger in Paradise.' But then they had to go and play 'Let's Get Drunk and Screw.' It was a sad reminder that it had been a long time since I'd…well, you know, that 'S' word.

Not that I hadn't had plenty of opportunities to fool around. But of all the men who'd offered to help me 'forget all about Randy,' I only found one attractive enough to sleep with.

Okay, that's a lie. I was drunk and he took advantage of it. He was a studio musician I'd worked with for years, and I was newly divorced, intoxicated, and eager to prove to myself that I no longer needed Randy. But instead of enjoying the experience, I felt guilty for having casual, meaningless sex. That's when I made a solemn vow to myself not to have intercourse with anyone unless I fell in love with them, which probably means I'll be celibate for the rest of my life, considering how most of the men I've met lately are either jerks, drug addicts, or both.

After I finished singing along with Jimmy about drinking and fornicating, I decided it was too much trouble to pour the wine into a glass. So I sipped the rest straight from the bottle. Maybe that's why I didn't think it was big deal when the glass fell off the hammock and shattered on the floor. In fact, I found it kind of humorous.

I drained the bottle, curled into a ball, and held it close to my breast like it was a baby.

Then everything did a crazy little spin around me and faded to black.

chapter 7

I WOKE UP the next morning, wishing I hadn't.

Hadn't drank so much, that is. And hadn't fallen asleep (okay, passed out) in the hammock. All I could do was lie there and gaze blankly at the porch's ceiling fan, spinning slowly in the breeze, and wonder why I had been dumb enough to drink an entire bottle of wine.

Speaking of being possessed, a demon had taken up residence inside my stomach. He was causing quite a stir in there, mixing up all the gastrointestinal juices and making me nauseous. Another demon had crawled inside my head and was using a jackhammer on my skull. I knew those two demons well and had made several promises to myself that I would never invite them back. Yet, here they were, up to their old tricks. All because of my stupidity. All because I thought I could drink my troubles away.

I raised my head. Big mistake. The demon in my belly took it as a cue to send all my stomach's contents up my throat and out my mouth.

I puked all over my sundress before I managed to roll on my side and aim for the floor.

"Sara!" I called out once the heaving ceased. "Please come here!"

Surely she would have mercy on her mother and help me clean up the mess I'd made, right?

Okay, maybe not, but it was worth a shot. Besides, I wanted the reassurance of knowing she was home. Especially after her little tantrum last night that drove me to drinking in the first place.

"Sara, honey, can you come here?" I hollered, hoping she'd be able to hear me through her bedroom window, which was just above the porch's roof.

No answer.

I gave up and swung my legs off the hammock. My bare feet hit the floor, and—

"Owww! Shiiiittttt!" I cried out in pain.

I sank back into the hammock and inspected my foot.

"You're such an ignoramus," I told myself as I watched blood ooze from the bottom of my heel. Like a dummy, I had stepped on a shard of the broken wine glass.

Great, I thought. *The morning's just begun and things are already going from bad to worse.*

I called for Sara again.

No reply.

I got up and hopped on my good foot to the kitchen, leaving drops of blood along the way.

I searched the 'junk' drawer by the sink for a Band-Aid but couldn't find one, so I grabbed a dishtowel and wrapped it around my foot to control the bleeding. I was tying it around my ankle to hold it in place, when the doorbell rang.

I hobbled over to the door and took a look through the peephole. What I saw made me wonder if I was really awake.

"No, it can't be," I whispered. "This has got to be some kind of nightmare."

The doorbell rang again. As much as I wanted to deny it, the boy who stood on the landing was real.

His hair was raven and spiked. Diamond earrings glittered in both his lobes. And he was wearing a Devil's Reject T-shirt and holy jeans. Worst of all, he held a suitcase in one hand and a duffle bag in the other.

My headache exploded with a newfound intensity.

"Anyone in there?" the boy called out.

For a moment I considered doing nothing, just to see if he would go away. But I knew he'd come all the way from California, so chances were good that he wouldn't give up that easily.

I grimaced and opened the door.

"Hey, Ms. Jenkins!" he greeted me cheerfully. "I was beginning to wonder if you guys were home."

I glared at him. What in blue blazes was he doing *here*?

"Are you okay, Ms. Jenkins?" he asked. "You look a little pale. And what happened to your dress? It's got a big stain all over the front of it."

I crossed my arms. "I puked it on it, Alex. I'm not feeling well."

"Oh, sorry to hear that," he said with a nervous laugh. His eyes lowered to my foot. "Oh, what happened there? It looks like you're bleeding."

I looked down. "Yeah. Funny thing...stepping on glass will do that to you."

"Wow, sounds like you're having a bad morning."

I looked him in the eye. "You have no idea. And it just got a whole lot worse. Would you mind telling me what you're doing here?"

"Why, Sara invited me," he said with a grin. "Didn't she tell you?"

I hate to admit it, but thoughts of murdering my daughter crept into my mind.

"No, she didn't mention it," I said. "Funny how she forgot to let me in on it."

He shrugged. "Well, anyway, here I am. I can spend the whole week with you guys. Isn't that awesome?"

"Totally," I said sarcastically.

He peered around me into the house. "You think I can come in, Ms. Jenkins? My things are getting kinda heavy."

What could I do? Send him back home? It wasn't like he lived around the corner.

"Sure, why not," I said in surrender.

He set his stuff down in the foyer and glanced around the house. "Nice little place, Ms. Jenkins. Sara told me it sucked, but I don't see why. Your view of the ocean is awesome."

"Thanks," I said, standing like a flamingo so I could take the weight off my injured foot. "So do you care to enlighten me on how you got here? I'm especially interested in the part about Sara inviting you."

He wiped a bead of perspiration from his brow. "Wow, it sure is humid here in South Carolina. First time I've been here, you know. Been to North Carolina…Charlotte, I think, but never to South Carolina. It kinda feels like Florida in a way. You know, real sticky and—"

"Alex! Focus on what I asked you…*how did you get here?*" Lord, he was testing my patience.

"Oh, that. Well, Sara told me she was bored here with just you around, so she invited me to come. I asked my dad and he said it was cool with him. He was flying to Florida with his new girlfriend anyway, so he took me along and had the pilot stop at the Charleston airport to let me out. Then I caught a cab. That's how I got here."

I made a mental note to have a long talk with Alex's dad when I got back to California. He was my record producer, and we'd known each other for years. Like me, he had recently divorced. Unlike me, he seemed happy about it. And from what I'd heard, he was spending quite a bit of the fortune he'd made in the music business on high-end prostitutes. So I was pretty sure the 'girlfriend' he was taking to Florida had come with a hefty price tag.

"It was so nice of your dad to drop you off and not even check in with me," I said, tongue in cheek. "And it was so nice of Sara to keep your visit a secret. I wonder what else she hasn't told me?"

He shrugged. "Beats me. Where is she, anyway?"

I tried to keep a straight face and said, "Sorry to tell you this, but she ran off with a lifeguard yesterday. Real hunky dude. It was love at first sight."

He looked at me like he wasn't sure if I was pulling his leg or not. "Oh, Ms. Jenkins, that's not true...*is it?*"

I shook my head. "Naw, I was just kidding. She really ran off with a bodybuilder. You should have seen his biceps."

He grinned. "Now I know you're messing with me. So where is she, really?"

I nodded toward the stairs. "Getting her beauty sleep, I suppose."

"Can I go wake her?"

Did he really think I was going to let him go barging into her room? What if she was sleeping in her skimpies? Get real.

"I'll go get her," I said. *And strangle her while I'm at it,* I thought.

As I limped up the stairs, I rehearsed the tongue lashing I was going to give Sara. If she thought having her phone taken away for a month was bad, she hadn't seen anything yet. Hell had no fury like a mother who suddenly found herself with an unwanted houseguest.

Sara's door was unlocked, so I threw it open. "Get up right now, young lady! We need to—"

Panic stuck in my throat when I realized I was talking to an empty bed; one that was made and had a guitar lying across it—in the same exact spot it had been last night when she'd stormed outside.

"Oh, my God," I gasped. "She never came home."

My heart pounded against my ribs as I rushed down the stairs, no longer aware of the pain in my foot, no longer aware of the headache or the churning in my stomach. All I could think of was Sara and all the bad things that might have happened to her.

"Ms. Jenkins, is something wrong?" Alex asked when I reached the bottom step.

I couldn't catch my breath. Between gasps, I said, "Yes... Sara didn't sleep...in her bed. She ran out on the beach last night because she was upset. I don't think she ever...came back."

"I'm sure she's okay, Ms. Jenkins," Alex said with surprising calm. "I bet she decided to sleep on the beach. I've done it before in California. That is, until the cops came along and told me I couldn't. I guess they've got some kind of regulation against—"

"Alex, shut up! I don't give a damn about any of that right now! Sara is missing and I'm scared to death! I can't even think straight!"

"You want me to go look for her?" he volunteered.

I was in tears now. "Sure. I guess that's a good idea."

He nodded, his expression becoming more somber. "Don't worry, Ms. Jenkins. Sara can take care of herself. Why don't you try to calm down while I go look for her outside. You look like you're going to have a heart attack or something."

I shooed him away with my trembling hands. "Just go, Alex! Go find her!"

"Yes, ma'am." He turned and hurried off.

Should I call the police? I wondered.

I searched for my phone but couldn't find it.

Think, dammit! Where did you put it?

I raced into my bedroom. *Didn't I put it on the charger last night? It should be sitting on my nightstand.*

It wasn't there.

I had to find it. I had to have in case I needed to—

I did a double take at my bed. It should have been made since I slept in the hammock last night. But the covers were turned down. And was that a mane of blonde hair flowing over one of the pillows?

Never before had I experienced such a dichotomy of emotions. Part of me wanted to smother the sixteen year-old girl sleeping in my bed with kisses. Another part of me wanted to scold her, to let her know that she had given me the worst scare a mother could have.

I settled for planting a kiss on her cheek and removing the earbuds from her ears. A rap song blasted from them. No wonder she never heard me calling for her.

"Wake up, sweetie," I said, giving her shoulder a gentle nudge.

"I want to sleep in," she mumbled. "Come back later."

I eased myself down on the side of the bed. "Not a good idea. Your boyfriend is here."

She shot straight up. "*He is?* You mean he's really, really here?"

"Yes, he's really, really here. And I think you have a lot of explaining to do."

She rubbed her eyes. "God, I didn't know he'd really do it. I mean, I told him I was bored and all, but I didn't think he'd really come."

"He said you invited him. Is that true?"

She looked confused. "No...well, maybe, yeah. I mean, I sorta suggested it. But I didn't think he took me seriously."

"Apparently he did. That's why you have to be careful what you say."

She wrinkled her nose. "Ewwww, Mom, you stink! You smell like puke!"

"Sorry, I've had a rough morning."

She studied my dress. "God, you *did* puke! All over yourself! Why'd you drink so much last night?"

"You know about that, huh?"

"Yeah, it was pretty obvious when I found you passed out in the hammock, clutching an empty bottle. That's why I got in your bed. I figured if you weren't going to use it, I was. It's a lot more comfortable than that thing up in my room."

"Ms. Jenkins?" Alex called out from the living room.

Sara leapt from the bed and ran to him. By the time I caught up with her, she had her arms wrapped around his neck, giving him a kiss on the lips—a kiss that lasted way too long in my opinion.

I cleared my throat. "Alex, why don't you take your things to the guest room and get settled."

Sara unhooked her arms from his neck and said, "Is he staying in the one upstairs?"

Yeah, right. Like I was born yesterday. Did she really think I'd tempt fate by putting him in the room next to hers? Not in this lifetime.

"No, he's staying in the one downstairs," I said. "Suzanne is coming and she prefers the one upstairs." It was a lie—Suzanne could care less where she slept, but at least it sounded like a reasonable excuse.

Sara's eyes opened wide. "Suzanne's coming? Cool! I love her soooo much!"

Great. She loves Suzanne but hates me. Where did I go wrong?

"Sara, show Alex his room," I said. "I'm going to take a shower, then we can all go down to the Lost Dog Café and get some breakfast."

A horn sounded outside.

Now what? I thought.

I hobbled to the kitchen to take a look out the window above the sink. Alex and Sara followed.

"Holy crap, look at that Hummer limo!" Alex exclaimed when I opened the mini-blinds.

It was parked in front of the house. My jaw fell as a news van and a black sedan nosed in behind it.

"Oh, no," I gasped. "What does she think she's doing?"

"Who is it?" Alex asked.

Sara answered for me. "It must be Suzanne! Yay! She's here!"

"And so is the media," I muttered, wondering what in the world I had done to deserve this day that, so far, had been sent straight from hell.

chapter 8

TEN MINUTES PASSED, and Suzanne still hadn't emerged from the limo.

"What's taking her so long?" Sara wanted to know.

I blew out a sigh. "She's probably checking her makeup and making sure every hair is in its proper place. She has to look good for the camera, you know."

Seconds later, two more vehicles came to a stop across the street. One was a van with 'Live Five News' emblazoned across its side. The other was a white sedan with a magnetic sign on the door that read *The Post and Courier.*

Great. More media. How on God's green earth did they know she was coming here? Surely Suzanne wouldn't have told them. If anyone knew how much I valued my privacy, it was her. It just didn't make any sense.

"I can't believe Suzanne Richardson is staying here," Alex said, pressing his forehead against the window. "She was so hot in *Revenge of the Pharos.* I dreamt about her for months after seeing that movie."

Sara slapped him across the shoulder and said, "Dude, not a cool thing to say in front of your girlfriend!"

"Sorry. But you have nothing to worry about. You're even hotter than she is." He gave her a kiss on the lips.

I cringed.

"Hey, wait, I think something's happening!" Sara said.

We watched the chauffer get out and walk the length of the cavernous Hummer, all the way to the passenger door at the rear. He waved to the reporters and cameramen who were closing in, and placed a white-gloved hand on the handle.

He hesitated for a moment, then pulled the door open.

A pair of shapely calves swung into the sunlight.

"Oh, wow, she's even hotter in person," Alex commented as Suzanne stood and straightened the black mini-dress she had managed to pour her voluptuous body into.

Reporters and cameramen formed a circle around her. She answered their questions, posed for some still shots, and signed a few autographs. When she was done with them, she blew everyone a kiss and strutted across the yard toward the house.

I hurried for the door. Sara and Alex joined me, and we all stood there, waiting expectantly, looking like a welcoming committee.

But I wasn't in a welcoming mood. I just wanted her to get inside so the media circus would pack up and leave. So as soon as I heard the click of her heels on the landing, I opened the door, grabbed her by the arm, and jerked her across the threshold.

One of her stilettos caught on the doorsill, causing her to stumble forward. Next thing I knew, she was lying face down on the floor.

I yelled for Alex to shut the door. Then I knelt beside Suzanne and asked her if she was okay.

She didn't say anything, nor did she move.

"C'mon, Suzanne, please tell me you're all right," I said, giving her shoulder a nudge.

She raised her head slowly and blew a strand of burgundy hair from her eyes. "Gee, it's great to see you, too, A.J. Thanks a lot for the warm welcome."

"I'm sorry, but I'm a little pissed off with you right now. Why in the world did you get the media to follow you out here?"

"I didn't. They just happened to be at the airport when I landed. They were waiting for the governor to arrive. But some of them spotted me and ended up following the limo out here. I can't help it if I'm famous, you know? Things like that happen."

Sara knelt beside me. "Hi, Suzanne," she said with a grin. "I'm really glad you came. Sorry you fell."

Suzanne's face lit up. "Hey, baby girl! I swear you get prettier every time I see you. I've got a present for you...you can open it as soon as your mom lets the chauffer in. He's carrying all my stuff up here."

There was a knock at the door. I assumed it was the chauffer so I asked Alex to open it.

But it wasn't the chauffer. It was a balding overweight photographer. Something told me he was paparazzi.

He barged right in and snapped a picture of Suzanne sprawled out on the floor.

"You no-good bastard!" she yelled, rising to her feet. "You show that picture to one person and I'll sue your ass!"

"Too late," the man said. "Can you imagine how much this is going to be worth? A photo of Suzanne Richardson, spread-eagled on the floor! God, it'll fetch me thousands!"

Suzanne lunged for him, but he was too quick for her. He darted out the door and ran down the stairs.

"If you make that picture public I swear I'll hunt you down and kill you!" she screamed from the doorway. "I know people in the mob! You want to end up at the bottom of the river? Or would you prefer decapitation?"

"Suzanne, shut the door," I said, trying to remain calm.

"I mean it, you piece of shit!" she continued. "You just wait—you'll regret you were born when I get through with you!"

The chauffer appeared at the door, shoulders slumped from the weight of the two suitcases he was holding. "Where would you like these, Ms. Richardson?" he asked.

"Take them upstairs," I answered for her, and told Sara to show him the way to the guest room.

"Bastard," Suzanne grumbled as she closed the door. "I can't believe that idiot got a picture of me on the floor. I bet my thong was showing." She turned, finding herself face to face with Alex. "Who's this?" she asked, pointing a finger at him.

"I'm Alex," he said, blushing. "I'm a big fan of yours, Ms. Richardson. You were awesome in *Return of the Pharos.*"

"Oh, that silly thing?" she said with a dismissive wave of her hand. "I only took the role as a favor to the screenwriter. I was dating him at the time. It wasn't worth it, though. He was terrible in bed; had to get a magnifying glass to find his pecker."

I cleared my throat. "Um, Suzanne, I don't think that's an appropriate thing to say in front of Alex."

"Alex, huh?" She smiled and gave him a hug. "I know you—you're the one Sara's been telling me about. I heard you two are a hot item."

Alex looked surprised. "Sara told you we were a hot item?"

Suzanne nodded. "Yep, she tells me everything." With a raspy laugh, she added, "And I mean *everything.*"

I made a mental note to find out what this *everything* business was all about.

Suzanne gave me a disgusted look. "Holy crap, girl, what happened to you? Your dress is stained and you smell like puke. Did you throw up?"

I nodded, embarrassed.

She eyed the towel wrapped around my foot. "And what kind of fashion statement is *that?*"

"Stepped on a broken wine glass," I said. "Tell you all about it later."

She shook her head. "You never could hold your alcohol, could you? Speaking of which—"

She went to the kitchen and opened the fridge. I followed her, knowing I was in for a tongue lashing.

"Hey, you didn't get the beer like I asked you to!" she said, turning to face me. How are we supposed to party?"

"I don't think it's a good idea for you to—"

She slammed the refrigerator door closed. "No lectures, A.J., I mean it! I can handle a few drinks just fine. I'm not an alcoholic, I just like to drink, that's all."

I rolled my eyes. "Yeah, I've heard that before—like the night you wound up in jail."

"I spent one night there, big deal. It was good publicity— helped my bad girl image, although we both know I'm an innocent sweetheart." She laughed and made her way to me. "It's good to see you, girl," she said, throwing her arms around me. "You know I love you. And we've got soooo much to catch up on. Why don't we take a little trip down to Bert's and get a couple of twelve packs so we can sit on the porch and talk?" She let go of me and made a face. "But first, take a shower. You stink to high heaven."

The chauffer came downstairs and asked Suzanne if she needed anything else.

"No, darlin', I'm good," she told him, and walked with him to the front door. She gave him a peck on the cheek and said, "I left a nice tip for you on the backseat. Use it to paint the town with."

"Yes, ma'am," he said with a boyish grin. "But that kiss you gave me is the best tip I ever got. I'll cherish it for the rest of my life."

She nodded. "My pleasure. And do me a favor—if you see that asshole photographer, kick his butt for me."

"Yes ma'am." He tipped his hat and made his exit.

Sara came bounding down the stairs. "Do you really have a gift for me?" she asked Suzanne.

"Sara, where's your manners?" I snapped.

Suzanne laughed. "It's okay, baby girl. I'll go upstairs and get it for you in a minute. But I'll tell you this much—it's something you told me you really, really wanted."

"Is it a MyFi?" Sara squealed.

Suzanne grinned. "Yep, it's a MyFi."

"What's a my-fly?" I asked, perplexed.

Suzanne and Sara burst into laughter. "It's not a my-fly," Suzanne said. "It's a MyFi. It's a personal satellite radio about the size of an IPod."

"Oh, I see," I said, still unsure what they were talking about. "You listen to music on it?"

Sara giggled. "Mom, you're so uncool. Of course, you listen to music on it. What else would you do with it?" She gave Suzanne a hug. "Thank you for getting it for me. And thank you for coming here to stay with us. It's been sooo boring with just Mom around. She's no fun."

I turned so they wouldn't see the tears welling in my eyes.

"Please excuse me," I said. "I'm going to take my shower now."

I went to my room, locked the door, and slipped out of my clothes. But I didn't head straight for the shower. Instead, I fell across the bed and reached for the notebook on my nightstand. With tears blurring my vision, I jotted down the lyrics to a new song that was jelling inside my head.

One about a mother who desperately wants to win back the affection of her daughter, no matter what it takes.

chapter 9

SUZANNE WAS AN expert at wearing down your resistance. So it wasn't long after I showered and dressed that she had me in the Jag, driving her to Bert's to get some beer.

She must have noticed my glum mood, 'cause about half-way there she stopped yapping about her latest sexual escapade and asked me what was wrong.

I put my finger to my chin like I had to mull it over. "Hmmm, can't think of anything right off hand," I said. "Although it could have something to do with the fact that my daughter hates me."

She cocked an eyebrow. "Hates you? Why would you think something like that?"

"Um, maybe because she tells me she hates me at least once a day. I'd say that's pretty good evidence she does, don't you?"

Suzanne waved me off. "Oh, hell, A.J., she's a kid—they say stuff like that but don't mean it. And if she really hates anything it's the divorce, not you. She's been taking it pretty bad, you know."

I felt like saying "No shit," but kept it to myself.

We drove the rest of the way in silence. When I reached Bert's I had to wait on a parking space, since there weren't that many of them and the store was packed with shoppers getting ready for the Fourth of July, which was only a day away. Finally, a rusty old neon pulled out of a slot and I zoomed into it, not wanting to take a chance on someone beating me to it.

"Damn, you're starting to drive like me!" Suzanne exclaimed as we came to a whiplash-inducing stop.

I undid my seatbelt but kept the engine running so the AC would keep us cool.

"So how do you know all this stuff about Sara?" I asked her. "Have you two been talking?"

She unhooked her seatbelt. "Yeah, she calls me from time to time to vent. She knows I'm a good listener."

I almost laughed out loud. *Good listener* wasn't exactly what came to mind when I thought of Suzanne.

"So what exactly does she say when she does this venting?" I asked.

She bit her lower lip. "I don't think I should tell you. She feels like she can confide in me. I don't want to betray her trust."

I narrowed my eyes at her. "I'm her mother. You should tell me *everything.*"

"Oh, it's nothing bad—if it was, I'd let you know. She's just confused right now, A.J. She hates not having her mom and dad together. I can relate because I was around her age when my folks split up. That's when I told my mom she could go to hell and left home, remember?"

I let out a sigh and asked, "So what am I supposed to do? Take Randy back just to make her happy? All he would do is turn around and cheat on me again."

"He's a rock star," Suzanne said. "You really didn't expect him to ignore all those women going crazy over him, did you? But I think he really loves you. He just—"

"Never grew up," I cut in. "And he never will. That's why I gave up on him."

She reached for the rearview mirror and turned it so she could check her face in it. "All I know is Sara feels like a rubber band," she said. "Do my eyes look red to you?"

"No, they look green. I wish my eyes were as pretty as yours."

"Ha, ha, you know what I mean—do my eyes look blood-shot?"

I scrutinized them and told her they looked fine.

"So what do you mean by Sara feeling like she's a rubber band?" I asked.

She took a bottle of eye drops from her purse. "She feels like a rubber band because you stretch her one way when you try to get her take your side." She reclined the seat and squeezed two drops into her left eye. "Then Randy comes along and stretches her the other way when he tries to get her to take his side." She squeezed two drops into her right eye. "The poor kid's going to break one day if ya'll don't stop it." She blinked a few times, then said, "Okay, let's get the friggin' beer!"

"Whoa, wait a minute," I said as she opened her door. "Aren't you going to disguise yourself? I've got hats and wigs in the trunk you can use."

She looked at me like I had lost my mind. "Why would I want to do that? I love to mingle with my fans. It's fun."

"But—"

She slid out and closed the door. I said a few naughty words under my breath and reached in the backseat for my baseball cap and sunglasses.

By the time I got them on she had already made her way to the store's entrance. I watched a couple come out, do a double-take at her, and follow her inside.

I mumbled a few more naughty words and got out the car.

I was halfway to the door when I noticed a poster taped to it. As I drew closer I realized it had something to do with the girls Mrs. Turner had told me about, the giveaway being the headline at the top that read: MISSING.

Below the headline was a photo of the girls. Both of them had long blonde hair and blue eyes. Their resemblance to Sara could only be described as uncanny.

A handwritten message below the photos read: *Please help us find these missing girls. Both were last seen walking on the beach near the county park. Call Crime Stoppers if you have any information on their whereabouts. A sizable reward is being offered and your call will be kept confidential.*

I peered again at the photos, read the names of the girls, and wondered how their parents were coping with such a horrible tragedy.

A tap on my shoulder startled me. I swiveled my head around and found a middle-aged woman wearing a scarf on her head standing behind me. "I don't mean to be rude," she said, "but I was wondering if you were planning on going inside sometime today?"

"I'm so sorry," I said, stepping out of her way. "I didn't mean to block the door. I was just—"

"Yeah, I know," she said, nodding at the poster. "It's a shame about those girls. But mark my words, they'll never find them alive. Someone's done raped and killed them for sure. And I bet who ever did it isn't finished yet. They'll be more to come."

"Well, I hope your wrong," I said, put off by her rotten attitude. "And I think we should all pray they're okay."

She shrugged and said, "To each their own," then went inside.

I took one more look at the photos. *Long blonde hair, blue eyes, cute up-turned noses.* They could be Sara's sisters.

It sent a shiver down my spine as I opened the door and went inside.

Not surprisingly, Suzanne was surrounded by shoppers. A few were taking pictures of her with their phones, others were finding whatever they could—napkins, paper towels, parts of their bodies—for her to autograph. I kept my distance and made my way to the bread aisle to get some hamburger buns.

I was sorting through the packages, trying to find the freshest offering, when someone behind me asked, "Any more flat tires?"

I spun around and found myself face to face with Dr. Drew, dressed casually in a pair of khaki shorts and a Parrot Head T-shirt. A few days of stubble peppered his face. And his eyes— God, they were so *blue*—bluer than I'd remembered.

"Fancy meeting you here," he said with a perfect smile. "Are you vacationing here at Folly?"

I had trouble finding my voice. When I finally did, I stuttered, "I...I'm...I'm staying at a beach house."

I felt like slapping myself on the forehead for saying something so dumb. Of course, I was staying at a beach house. What other kind of house was there on the beach? But there was something about Dr. Drew that made me nervous and unable to think straight.

"How cool is that?" he said. "I just bought a house here a few weeks ago. What a coincidence."

"Yeah, what a coincidence," I said.

"The house I bought isn't much, but I got it for a real steal," he went on to say. "It's a little cottage near the west end of the beach. Are you near the west end too?"

I nodded. "Yeah. Not far from the county park."

"Looks like we're practically neighbors, then."

I inhaled his cologne—it was the same kind Randy wore. Gucci.

"Is something wrong?" Dr. Drew asked.

I shook my head, trying to clear my jumbled thoughts. "I…I was just about to grab some buns."

Oh, my God, that sounded so bad, I thought.

His face creased into a smile. "You were, huh?"

Blood rushed to my cheeks. "I meant hamburger buns," I said. "You know, the kind you put hamburgers on."

"I assumed that's the kind of buns you were referring to." He inched closer. "Can I ask you something? Why do you always wear that baseball cap and those big honking sunglasses?"

"I…I'm very sensitive to the sun," I said, groping for an excuse. "I break out in hives if I get too much UV exposure."

"But you're inside," he pointed out.

"Can't be too careful. Not with sensitive skin like mine."

"If you say so." He reached around me. "Please excuse me, but I need to grab some buns too." He gave me wink. "I'm having a cookout party on the Fourth at my house. Would you and Sara like to come?"

I stepped aside so he could rummage through the buns without me being in the way. "Oh, I'm afraid not. I've got company and have to entertain them. You know how it is."

"Bring them with you," he suggested.

"Oh, you wouldn't want them to come," I said. "They tend to get a little...rowdy."

"I like rowdy people," he said. "They keep me in business."

I wasn't sure what he meant at first. Then it dawned on me. "Oh, you mean because they break their bones?"

"Yep. The rowdier the better. So why don't you haul them down to my house for the cookout."

Just then, an explosion of laughter erupted from the shoppers gathered around Suzanne. Dr. Drew nodded in her direction and said, "You got any idea what that's all about? Who's that woman everyone is flocked around?"

"Have no idea," I said. "Probably some spokesmodel for one of the products the store carries. You know how they always get sexy women to sell stuff."

"But in *here?*" He made a wide sweeping gesture of the store with his hand. "I could see something like that happening in a big supermarket, but in this little joint?"

I shrugged. "Like I said, I dunno."

The crowd suddenly parted. Suzanne walked our way. My heart raced.

"C'mon, A.J., let's get my beer," she said when she reached us.

Dr. Drew's mouth dropped open. "You're...you're *Suzanne Richardson,*" he gasped.

She rolled her eyes. "Thanks for letting me know. I have this amnesia problem and forget who I am sometimes. Thanks to people like you, I never have to worry about remembering my name." She looked at me and said, "Who's this guy, anyway?"

"This is Dr. Drew," I said. "He helped me with a flat tire on the way to the beach."

She grinned. "Cool. Any friend of A.J.'s is a friend of mine." She extended her hand. "Nice to meet you, Dr. Drew."

"Nice to meet you too." He cut his eyes at me. "So you're A.J., huh? As in A.J., the famous singer-songwriter?"

I shrugged. "Afraid so. That's why I wear the hat and sunglasses. I like to keep a low profile in public."

"Well, your secret is safe with me," he said. "You know, I'm a big fan of yours. I bet I've got every record you've made, going all the way back to the nineties." He shook his head. "I knew there was something familiar about you. How could I have missed it?"

For a moment we gazed at each other without speaking. Finding it awkward, I said, "Well, I guess I better grab my buns and go."

"And my beer," Suzanne reminded me.

"My offer for you to come to the cookout still stands," Dr. Drew said as I took a package from the shelf. "Bring Suzanne with you," he added. "Man, I can only imagine the looks on my guests' faces when two celebrities show up."

"That's nice of you. But like I said, I already have plans."

"You do?" Suzanne said with a quizzical look. "I think the cookout thing sounds kinda fun. Maybe we should go."

I grabbed her by the arm and dragged her toward the beer aisle. "Bye, Dr. Drew, it was nice to see you," I said over my shoulder. "Maybe we'll run into each other again."

"I hope so," he said, flashing another brilliant smile. "And I think you ought to listen to your friend and come to the cookout."

When we got to the beer section Suzanne asked me, "Why were you so rude to that guy? He's gorgeous. Don't you want to—"

"Shut up. Just shut up," I snapped.

"But he's got the hots for you, girl. And with his looks, you ought to have the hots for him too. Plus he's a freakin' doctor. What more could you want?"

"I said shut up. Now get your beer and let's get out of here."

She got two twelve-packs of Michelob Lite and carried them to the checkout counter.

That's when all hell broke loose.

It began when she spotted the new issue of *Star* magazine on a rack by the counter. As luck would have it, her picture was on the cover. It was anything but flattering.

"Shit!" she cried out. "Now they're saying I'm using crack cocaine!" She set her beer down on the checkout counter and started to rip the covers off the magazines. "Lies! It's all lies! You can't believe anything these assholes print! I've never done cocaine in my life and I never will!"

"Suzanne, please calm down," I said.

"Hell no, I'm not calming down! I'm sick of this shit! They can say anything they want and everyone believes them! It's just not fair!"

"It goes with the territory. They do it to all us, you know that."

She tossed all the magazines—now minus their covers—on the checkout counter. "I'm buying every one of these," she let the stunned cashier know, a girl who couldn't have been much older than Sara. "Then I want you to throw them in the trash where they belong. Better yet, *burn* the stupid things!"

"Yes, ma'am," the cashier said. After she rang up the magazines, beer, and buns, she gave us the total. It was a lot less than the five-hundred-dollar bill Suzanne handed her.

"Keep the change," Suzanne told her. "I'm sorry I blew up and said those bad words around you. I hope I didn't offend you."

The cashier was all grins now. "You can offend me anytime you want, Ms. Richardson. Especially if it means I get a tip like this!"

Suzanne smiled, told the girl she was pretty, and suggested she try a career in acting.

We were almost out the door when the girl called out, "Oh, and don't forget to keep your eyes open for those two girls who are missing. They're asking us to remind everyone."

"What girls?" Suzanne asked me.

"I'll tell you about it later," I said, reminding myself to keep a close watch on Sara for the rest of our stay.

chapter 10

SARA AND ALEX spent the afternoon surfing. Suzanne and I watched them from the screen porch, where we cheered Sara on in her quest to put Alex to shame; something she had no problem doing.

"She's awesome," Suzanne commented. She was sprawled across the wicker loveseat, looking relaxed in a bikini top and a pair of shorts. "I guess Randy taught her how to surf, huh?"

"Yeah," I said from the hammock. "That's Randy for you. Either playing the guitar or surfing." *Or fooling around with one of his groupies*, I felt like adding.

"So what's he up to these days?" Suzanne asked.

I shrugged. "I dunno. All I've heard is he's supposed to cut another album sometime soon. But if it doesn't do any better than the one that's out right now, it might be his last."

"He ought to go into acting," she said. "He's got the looks. Girls are always throwing their panties at him when he's playing on stage."

"Yeah, and I bet they give him a lot more than their panties after the show," I mused. "But it doesn't matter. He can screw every girl he wants to from now on. I'm over him."

"Yeah, right. You're a terrible actress, you know that?"

"What do you mean?"

"I mean you're far from over him. You can fool yourself but you can't fool me, kiddo."

"You're full of it," I said, watching Sara and Alex wade out of the surf and hop across the hot sand to a blanket near the dunes. When they got within hollering range, I cupped my hands around my mouth and shouted, "Hey, you guys better put some lotion on! The sun is really strong today!"

Sara put her surfboard down and looked my way. "We're fine," she shouted back. "Did you see me whip Alex's butt in our contest to see who could stay on their board the longest? He's such a crappy surfer. They'd laugh him off the beach in Malibu." She put her arms around his waist and kissed him on the cheek. "But I still love him!"

"Aw, they're so sweet," Suzanne said. "I think they make such a cute couple."

"Cute my butt," I grumbled. "They're too young to be acting so serious."

"Oh, chill out, will you? First loves are special—let her enjoy it while she can."

"I don't know. I worry about her."

"Worry, worry, worry, that's all you ever do. Jeez, A.J., you need to lighten up and have some fun. And some sex."

I shot her a surprised look. "I beg your pardon?"

"You heard me. When's the last time you were with a man?"

"Hmm...let's see, I was with one today. I was standing beside him at Bert's, remember?"

"Very funny. You know what I mean—when was the last time you were with a man in the biblical sense?"

"I believe about the same time Moses parted the Red Sea. Or maybe it was back when Noah was rounding up all those animals."

Suzanne got up from the loveseat. "I'm getting us some beer. Then we're going to discuss this in more detail."

"I don't want to discuss it in more detail. And I don't want—"

She took off without listening to me. When she returned, she handed me a Michelob. I crinkled my nose and told her, "I don't like this stuff. I prefer wine."

"You don't have any wine, so take it."

She went back to the loveseat and lowered herself gracefully into it. "Beer's good for your heart, you know," she said as she twisted the cap off. "And other things too...but I can't remember what they are."

"I heard it's bad on your liver." I took a sip and made a face. "Ugh! I've never like this stuff since you made me chug it back in high school."

Suzanne laughed. "Those were the good old days, weren't they? We had so much fun at this beach."

"Yeah," I said. "Until..."

She nodded sadly. "Yeah, until..."

A silence fell over us.

Suzanne was the first to break it by saying, "Hey, I'm sorry if I got you to thinking about bad stuff."

"It's okay," I said with a forced smile. "That's why I go to therapy—to learn how to deal with it." I took another sip of beer. "But let's talk about something else, okay?"

Her face brightened. "Sure. Let's get back to talking about sex. Just when do you plan on getting laid again?"

Leave it to Suzanne to be so blunt. But it was one of the things I secretly admired about her.

"I'm not looking to get laid," I said. "At least not until I find the right guy."

"Oh, pleassseee don't start that right guy shit with me! You need to get laid ASAP. If I were you, I'd go find that doctor who has the hots for you and play nurse with him."

"Don't be ridiculous. I don't think he has the hots for me."

"You're blind then. He wants you, kiddo. It was written all over his face. So let him do you a favor and give you an orgasm or two. You'll feel much better afterwards."

"I'm not into causal sex," I said.

"The way I see it, you're not into *any* kind of sex right now. Don't you miss it?"

I shrugged. "Maybe...a little...sometimes."

"Liar! You're thirty-five, that means you're at your sexual peak. You need someone to satisfy you at least a couple of times a week. If you don't, you're going to turn into a real bitch."

"Sara already thinks I'm a bitch."

"See? What I tell you? That's why you're going to that doctor's cookout even if I have to drag you down there kicking and screaming."

"I don't even know where he lives," I pointed out. "So I couldn't go if I wanted to."

"Oh, you want to. I saw how you looked at him. Can't blame you, either, he's a real hottie."

"He is good-looking," I admitted. "But I don't think a doctor would want to get involved with a celebrity. It just seems like a clash of cultures."

"Involved? Who said anything about getting involved? Just have sex with him." She took a swallow of her Michelob and added, "Besides, if you don't, I will."

I took the pillow from behind my head and threw it at her.

"See there?" she said, ducking just in time to keep it from hitting her in the face. "You're jealous."

"Am not. But you stay away from him. He's too nice of a guy for a bad girl like you."

"Yoo-hoo!" someone called out. I raised my head and saw Mrs. Turner standing at the screen door, cradling a watermelon.

I hopped out of the hammock and hurried to the door to open it for her.

"Hello, A.J.," she said. "I bought this for you and Sara. Can't have a decent stay at the beach without some watermelon to feast on."

I laughed. "Thank you so much, Mrs. Turner. Won't you come in for a while?"

"Don't mind if I do." She stepped inside and took a look around the porch. Her mouth fell open when she spotted Suzanne.

"Oh, my stars!" she exclaimed. "You're Suzanne Richardson!" The watermelon slipped from her hands and hit the floor with a thud.

"Damn, I didn't mean to frighten you," Suzanne said.

"I love all your movies," Mrs. Turner said, rushing toward her. "Especially *Return of the Pharaohs*. I must have seen it a hundred times."

Suzanne looked at me. "Why does everyone like that crappy movie? I thought I was much better in *The Mistress's Revenge*."

Mrs. Turner sat down next to her, obviously star-struck. I turned my eyes to the shattered watermelon. Thankfully, a few chunks looked intact enough to eat, so I excused myself and went to the kitchen to get a Tupperware bowl to put them in.

"I'll salvage what I can," I announced when I returned to the porch. "I'll wash the good pieces off. There should be enough for all of us."

"I'm so sorry," Mrs. Turner said. She was still seated next to Suzanne, giving her admiring glances. "I was just so shocked to see my favorite movie star in real life that I lost all my senses."

"No problem," I said. "Happens to everyone."

A few moments later, I served Suzanne and Mrs. Turner slices of the ill-fated watermelon. Then I settled back into the hammock to enjoy my own.

"Who's that boy Sara's been surfing with today?" Mrs. Turner asked me. She spit a seed out onto her plate.

"His name's Alex," I said. "He's visiting for a while."

"Sara's such a pretty girl," she said. "And she's so polite and well-mannered. Not many teens show the respect for their elders that she does."

I almost choked on my watermelon—she had to be talking about someone else's kid, right?

"You're so lucky to have a girl like that," Mrs. Turner went on to say. "I always dreamed of having one, but my husband and I were never able to conceive. Back in my day, they didn't have all them fancy things that can help you get pregnant like they do now."

"You mean like Viagra?" Suzanne said.

Honestly, she could be such a ditz sometimes.

"Heavens no," Mrs. Turner said with a laugh. "Viagra wouldn't have solved our problem. My husband was always horny and never had a problem getting it up. No, I'm afraid he was sterile."

"Oh," Suzanne said. "Well, why didn't you adopt a child, then?"

"My husband, rest his soul, didn't want to adopt. He said he would never be able to love someone else's child. I thought he was being stubborn, and we got in many an argument because of it, but I guess he ended up winning."

"That's a shame," Suzanne said.

"I'll tell you what's a shame," Mrs. Turner said. "Them poor missing girls, that's what. I can't imagine what their parents must be going through. I just seen one of the mothers on TV begging whoever had her daughter to let her go. Made me cry like a baby."

"So they don't have any idea who abducted them?" I asked.

"They ain't got a clue. And they're afraid whoever it is will strike again. They think he might be a serial killer or something. It's just plain dreadful."

"What are ya'll talking about?" Suzanne asked. "Has this got something to do with those girls I saw on the poster at Bert's?"

Mrs. Turner filled her in on the girls' disappearances. When she finished, Suzanne looked at me and said, "I can't believe something like that would happen out here on Folly. It's always been a pretty safe place, hasn't it, A.J.?"

I swallowed a bite of watermelon and said, "Oh, gosh, yeah. Me and my sister and brother used to roam this beach day and night. Mom and Dad never worried because they knew nothing bad would happen to us."

"Well I hope they catch whoever is doing it," Mrs. Turner said. "I can't sleep at night for worrying about it. I used to leave my windows open and let the sea breeze cool my house, but not anymore. Not until they catch that bastard."

"I know one thing," I said. "I'm not about to let Sara out of my sight. I noticed both the missing girls were blondes with blue eyes. Maybe the guy who took them has a thing for girls like that."

"Freakin' pervert," Suzanne said. "I'd like to get a hold of him and cut his nuts off."

Mrs. Turner nodded in agreement. "I'm with you, sister. And I'd be glad to hold him down, hand you the knife, and hang his nuts in a tree for the squirrels to nibble on when you're done."

Sundown found the three of us still lounging on the porch, chatting and drinking more beer than we should have.

I guess that's why I was feeling a little buzzed when Mrs. Turner brought up the subject of men and how rotten they were. She began by telling us how her husband used to cheat on her and how he would spend hundreds of dollars a month at strip clubs. Suzanne chimed in and shared lots of dirty laundry on her ex-husband and her most recent ex-lover. Then she looked at me, no doubt waiting for me to add to the tell-all.

But I didn't. Instead, I excused myself, explaining there was something I had to check on.

"Bring us another round of beers on your way back," Suzanne said. I noticed she was beginning to slur her words.

"Sure," I said, and took off for the living room.

The 'something' I wanted to check on was Sara and Alex. They were snuggled together on the sofa, watching a *Lord of the Rings* DVD. The purpose of my reconnaissance mission was to make sure their snuggling was 'G' rated and hadn't advanced to 'R' rated, so I kept my eyes cut in their direction while I made my way to the kitchen.

"Hey, do you know where the Solarcaine is?" Sara asked when she spotted me.

I stopped, looked over my shoulder, and said, "It's in the same place I always keep it."

"Where's that?"

"In the medicine cabinet in my bathroom."

"Could you get it for me? Me and Alex got burnt today."

Didn't I warn them they were going to get burnt if they didn't put more lotion on? And why did she expect *me* to get the Solarcaine? Didn't she have two perfectly good legs?

I sighed and trudged off to the medicine cabinet. On the way back to the kitchen, I tossed the bottle of Solarcaine to Sara.

"Hey! Wait!" she cried. "Aren't you going to spray me down? I need you to do my back!"

I sprayed her back and Alex's. Then I took three beers out the fridge and returned to the porch.

"Thank you, dear," Mrs. Turner said as I handed her a bottle. "Suzanne was just about to tell me how you got started in the music business. I've read stuff about it but she says it's not the whole story."

I gave Suzanne a look—one that meant she better keep her lips sealed, *or else.*

"I don't think Mrs. Turner would be interested in the *whole* story," I said as I handed Suzanne a beer.

"But it's such a cool story," Suzanne insisted, apparently too drunk to heed my non-verbal warning. "You see, she owes her career to me. I'm the one who got her discovered."

"You were?" Mrs. Turner said in surprise.

I fell into the hammock, wishing Suzanne would just shut up.

"Yeah, it's all because of me," she said proudly, then burped. "You see, she was really shy and dorky when she young, but I found out she was one hell of a songwriter and a damn good singer. So one night, when I was singing in a band in Charleston and A.J. came to see me, I got her good by singing one of the songs she wrote really *bad*. I mean, I sucked big time—on purpose, of course. I wanted to see if I could get her so upset that she'd want to come up on the stage and show everyone how it was supposed to sound. And it worked—especially since she had been drinking and had lost some of her inhibition."

"Suzanne, she doesn't need to know all that," I said.

She ignored me and said, "Anyway, there just so happen to be this talent scout dude there, and when he found out A.J. wrote the song and he heard how good she could sing, he asked her to do a demo. That's how she got a recording contract."

Okay, I thought, if she leaves it there it won't be so bad. But please, please don't get into the stuff about—

"The whole thing almost fell apart, though," Suzanne continued.

Crap. She was going to tell her *everything*.

Suzanne rattled on, "When she was making her first record she found out she was—"

"Stop! That's enough!" I cried.

"Let me finish," she shot back. "Anyway, she found out she was pregnant. Well, the record company had a cow—they didn't think an unwed knocked-up eighteen year-old would project a positive image or sell many albums, so they told her to get an abortion. But she told them no way. It almost cost her her career, but they let her wait until after she had Sara to cut her first album."

"Oh, my stars!" Mrs. Turner said. "I never knew any of this!"

I was ready to give Suzanne a piece of my mind for divulging something so personal. But before I had a chance to, I heard Sara say, "Interesting story, Mom. Funny how you never told me about it."

I sat straight up in the hammock. Sara stood in the doorway with her arms crossed. "I was going to ask you what was for dinner," she said. "But I've suddenly lost my appetite."

"Sara, let me explain," I said.

She turned and went inside.

I took off after her, wondering if she'd be able to forgive me for lying to her about her birth.

chapter 11

"GO AWAY! LEAVE me alone!" Sara cried from the other side of her bedroom door.

"We have to talk about this. Please let me in," I said.

It took a few minutes, but she finally unlocked the door.

She threw herself across the bed as I walked in.

"Honey, I'm so sorry this happened," I said, struggling to find the right words. "I was going to tell you the truth. I just wanted to wait until you were older."

"So is that why Daddy married you?" she said between sobs. "Is it because you got knocked up and he felt like he had to?"

I sat on the edge of the bed. "Of course not. Your dad married me because we were in love. And he loved you too. Long before you were born, just like me."

"Why did you tell me you got pregnant right after you and daddy got married? Why did you lie to me?"

"Because I didn't want you to know I had sex before I should have. I was only seventeen...eighteen, actually. It happened on my birthday."

"That's why you're always bitching at me about sex, isn't it? You're afraid I'm going to get knocked up like you did?"

I nodded. "I suppose that's part of it. But you have to realize something, honey. It happened when my world was falling apart. I'd just lost my mom and dad and my siblings. I was an emotional wreck. I guess I thought sex would somehow fill the void they left. But I was wrong."

"You should have got an abortion like those people wanted you to. You would have done me a favor."

Tears spilled down my cheeks. "Don't say something so horrible. You're the most precious thing on earth to me. I wish you would realize that."

"I want you to leave," she said, covering her face with a pillow. "I don't want to talk about it anymore."

"But, honey, I—"

"Just go away!"

I rose from the bed and started for the door. "Okay, I'm leaving. But I just want you to know I love you. No matter what, I'll always love you."

I closed the door behind me, leaned my back against it, and slid to the floor. With my head cradled in my hands, I wept.

I was still crying when a shadow fell over me.

"Are you okay?" Suzanne asked.

"Do I look okay?" I said without looking up at her.

"I'm really sorry for what happened," she said, lowering herself next to me. "I don't know what made me bring up all that stuff up about you getting pregnant around Mrs. Turner. I was way out of line. I guess I was—"

"You were drunk!" I snapped. "You're always drunk. That's why you're always doing stupid things. But you don't care, do you? You think it's funny. Well, it's not! You're a goddamn alcoholic. You hear me, Suzanne? You're a goddamn alcoholic. And I'm sick of it!"

Her eyes turned misty. "What do you want me to do? *Leave?*"

I didn't say a thing.

Instead, I got up and left, leaving it up to her to decide that for herself.

chapter 12

I WOKE THE next morning to a room ablaze with sunshine. A glance at the alarm clock told me it was early, only seven, so why did it look like high noon?

I raised my head and squinted out the window facing the beach. No wonder it was so bright—I had forgotten to close the mini-blinds when I went to bed. Now the sun, intensified by its reflection off the ocean, was illuminating my room like a spotlight.

I let my head sink back on the pillow and pulled the covers over my eyes. Maybe I could go back to sleep, just another hour or so. It wouldn't take much to lull me, especially with the peaceful sound of the waves breaking on the shore, the distant call of the gulls, the baby snores—

Baby snores? What the...

I jerked the covers down and discovered I wasn't alone.

Sara was lying next to me, her eyelids twitching from what must have been a pleasant dream, judging by the broad smile on her lips.

She looked so angelic, almost child-like in her silk PJ's. For several moments I watched the little movements she made, like opening and closing the palm of her hand as if she were grasping something. I wondered why she had crawled into bed with me, especially after everything that had happened last night. But I didn't want to dwell on that; it was too nice having her here, calm and peaceful; no arguing, no yelling. Just like it used to be when she was a child.

The smile faded on her lips. Her leg jerked and she moaned.

Looked like the pleasant dream was turning into a nightmare.

"No," she murmured, turning her head from side to side. "Don't let them get me."

"No one's going to get you," I whispered. "It's just a bad dream, honey."

"They're going to get me. They're going to kill me."

"No one's going to get you," I said in a soothing voice.

She became more agitated, flailing her arms about. "Get away! Don't you touch me! Let me go!"

I nudged her shoulder. "Sara, you're having a nightmare. Wake up."

"I know karate! I swear, I'll kill you if you touch me!"

"Baby, it's a dream. Wake up."

She raised an arm, made a fist, and took a swing in my direction.

Her fist landed squarely on my right eye.

"Owwww! Holy crap!" I cried out.

Sara's eyes flew open and she shot straight up.

"What happened?" she asked. "Why are you yelling, Mom?"

"You punched me," I said, holding my hand over my eye. "I bet it's going to turn black and blue."

"Oh, my God, I'm so sorry!" She forced my hand away to take a look. "Oh crap, Mom, I didn't mean to hurt you! I was swinging at those dudes who were trying to get me. It was such a scary dream."

"I know you didn't mean to hurt me," I said, "but I think you better get something cold to put on it so it doesn't swell."

"Like what?"

"I don't know…get a bag of mixed vegetables out of the freezer. That's what your grandma put on my bruises when I was little."

"How about a package of black-eyed peas?" she suggested with a giggle. "Wouldn't that be more appropriate?"

"Very funny. Now please hurry."

She returned in no time with the bag of veggies. I dabbed my eye with it and asked her, "So why were you in my bed in the first place?"

She answered with a shrug. "Just felt like it."

"Uh-huh. And *why* did you feel like it?"

She sat next to me on the bed and brought her knees to her chest. "I dunno. I couldn't sleep. I kept having bad dreams."

"I'll say."

"All night long I kept dreaming about a bunch of ugly dudes chasing me. I think they might have been demons or something. They smelled really bad too—kinda like you did yesterday morning with that puke all over your dress."

"Thanks for reminding me."

"Anyway, it was that, and…" Her voice trailed off.

"And what?" I probed.

She sighed. "Okay, it's like this…Suzanne had a long talk with me last night. She told me I've been acting like a brat lately and that I should treat you better. I got to thinking about it and realized she was sorta right. I also got to thinking about you not getting an abortion when you found out you were knocked up with me. Did you really put your music career on the line because of it?"

I nodded. "Yep. Although I really never thought of it that way. All I knew was I wanted to have you, no matter what."

"Why?"

Such a simple question. Such a complex answer.

I took a moment to search for the right words, then said, "Sara, there are things—things you might consider weird—that surround your birth. The day will come when I'll explain it all to you. And even though you'll think I've gone off the deep end when I do, I hope you'll come to understand it like I have."

She looked at me curiously. "Why the big secret? Why can't you tell me now?"

"I don't think you're ready for it. So just trust me on this one, okay?"

She gave me a reluctant nod. "Whatever. Anyway, I just want to let you know I think it's kinda cool that you stuck to your principles and all that stuff and didn't let anyone talk you into sucking me out of your womb." She leaned over and kissed my cheek. "Thanks."

Tears burned my eyes. "You're welcome."

"Mom, don't cry."

"I can't help it," I sobbed.

"Stop!" She fanned her face. "You're making me cry too!"

I was about to reach over and give her a hug, when the door flew open and Suzanne waltzed in.

"Hey! Ya'll want to go for a jog?" she asked.

She was certainly dressed for a jog—in a slutty sort of way. Short—and I mean short—fleece shorts and a sports bra that had to be a size too small for her boobs.

"I want to go!" Sara said.

"Cool," Suzanne said. "Do you have one of those scrunchy things? I want to put my hair in a ponytail so—" She shot me a puzzled look. "Hey, why are you holding that Jolly Green Giant bag to your eye? And why are you crying?"

"Sara punched me," I explained.

Her mouth dropped. "Damn, you guys are getting kinda violent, aint ya?"

"It was an accident," I said. "She hit me while she was having a nightmare."

Suzanne winked at Sara. "So you slept with your Mom, huh?"

Sara grinned and looked away. "I was scared. I kept having bad dreams."

"Uh-huh. And I suppose it had nothing to do with the talk we had, huh?"

Sara blushed and said nothing.

Suzanne smiled. "Anyway, I want to hit the beach before it gets crowded. You want to go with us, A.J.?"

I pointed to my eye. "Like this? Don't think so."

"Let me see what it looks like."

She came over and took the bag from my eye.

"Holy moly," she gasped. "You're going to have one hell of a shiner!"

"Great," I muttered.

"You better not let the paparazzi see you like this. They'll have a heyday. They'll come up with all kind of crap about you being the victim of domestic violence. Better keep your sunglasses on at all times."

"Thanks for the advice," I said as she handed me the bag back.

"Anyway, get dressed," she told Sara. "Like I said, I want to get my jog in before it gets too crowded to run. It's the Fourth, you know?"

Sara started for the door, but then stopped and looked over her shoulder at me. "Mom, I lied to you about something too," she said, pulling her pajama bottoms down to expose her tattoo. "This thing's a fake—it's a henna. I was just messing with you about it being real. I guess I did it because I was pissed off with you."

She giggled, pulled her bottoms back up, and took off.

Suzanne chuckled. "Looks like she got you good, huh?"

I joined her laughter, relieved to know my daughter wasn't as rebellious as I had thought.

"Looks like things are improving between you two," Suzanne said, checking out her own butt in the mirror above the dresser. "Looks like my little talk with Sara did some good."

"Yeah, she told me about that. Whatever you said sure made a difference."

"Glad I could help. You think I need a butt job?"

It was amazing how quickly she could change subjects. "I think your butt is fine."

"I want to make it rounder and fuller. Anyway, you sure you don't want to take a jog with us?"

"Suzanne, my eye hurts too much to do that. Ya'll go and have fun. But promise me you won't cause any scenes."

"Promise."

"And wear a big floppy hat and some sunglasses so people won't know who you are."

"If you insist."

"And…" I paused, thinking back to last night. "And I just want to let you know I'm sorry for saying those things to you in the hallway. I didn't mean it."

"I know," she said with a smile. "I know you love me, so no harm done."

Sara burst into the bedroom wearing a pair of cut-off shorts and a T-shirt. "I'm ready," she said. "Alex is going too. He's waiting on the porch."

Before they left I told Suzanne, "Make sure you don't let Sara out of your sight. I'm worried about all that stuff going on with the missing girls."

"Mom!" Sara protested. "I'm not a kid! I don't need someone watching me!"

"I'll keep my eye on her," Suzanne said. She put her arm around Sara and added, "Nothing will happen to this girl while I'm around. Of that you can be certain."

chapter 13

I SPENT MOST of the Fourth of July inside the house while Sara, Alex, and Suzanne frolicked on the beach. I wanted to join them but my bruised eye was so sensitive to light that it hurt to be outside. Thankfully, around three in the afternoon, a thick overcast rolled in which made the outside world bearable. So I grabbed the darkest pair of sunglasses I owned, tossed on a wide-brimmed floppy hat, and scooted out the door.

I found my motley crew riding the waves on boogie-boards. Sara spotted me from waist-deep water and shouted, "Hey, Mom! You gonna join us? The surf's really kicking up today!"

I pointed to my clothes—a T-shirt and a pair of shorts—not exactly boogie-boarding attire. "I'm not wearing a bathing suit under these," I hollered back. "I'm going to take a walk."

Sara looked puzzled. "Why do you want to talk?"

I laughed. The crashing surf must have made it hard for her to hear. "I said I'm taking a walk," I repeated. "I'll be back in a little bit."

She nodded and paddled out to deeper water. Suzanne and Alex followed her on their boards, and I stuck around long enough to watch them ride a few waves, wondering how many times Suzanne was going to have to adjust her bikini top to keep it from falling off.

"Okay, ya'll be careful," I said as I waved goodbye to them. "It's jellyfish season, you know. Don't get stung."

It didn't take long for me realize I had picked the wrong day to take a walk. The holiday had brought so many visitors to the beach that there was hardly a square foot of sand that wasn't occupied by someone lying on a blanket or reclining in a lounge chair. And the kids—good Lord, they were *everywhere*. One little boy ran in front of me, causing me to turn so sharply to keep from colliding with him that I nearly fell. To add insult to injury he had the nerve to tell *me* to watch where I was going. I gave his parents, who were drinking beer with a bunch of other thirty-somethings, a dirty stare. They shrugged and went back to partying.

After a while, I took off my flip-flops and let the sand ooze between my toes as I weaved in and out of the crowd toward the fishing pier. It was where we planned on watching the fireworks show tonight. Stretching over a thousand feet into the Atlantic, it offered the best vantage point to catch the town's annual pyrotechnics extravaganza—something I was looking forward to since there was a rumor circulating that this year's show would be the most spectacular in Folly's history.

The closer I got to the pier, the narrower the beach became, which made it more difficult to walk without having to step over a sunbather. So I finally gave up and turned around.

That's when I heard someone call out, "Hey, A.J.!"

I stopped and scanned the beach. Some guy was waving his arms to get my attention.

I squinted and realized it was Dr. Drew.

I waved back, admiring how good he looked without a shirt on as he made his way toward me.

"I saw you walking by and wanted to say hello," he said when he reached me. He smiled—that damn boyish, charming smile that reminded me so much of Randy. "So what are you up to?"

"Just taking a little stroll," I said, surprised that he recognized me in my silly floppy hat.

He gestured toward a large blue umbrella planted in the sand near the dunes. "Would you care to join me in the shade for a beer?" he asked.

"Um, I thought you said you were having some sort of party today?" I said, remembering what he had told me at Bert's. "But I only see one chair underneath your umbrella."

A stiff breeze rustled his sun-bleached locks. "Change of plans," he said. "I'll tell you all about it if you join me."

A debate began inside my head: *Should I do it or should I come up with some lame excuse why I have to go?*

The lame excuse thing was about to win. But then he took off his sunglasses. One look at those baby blues had me saying, "Okay, I guess I can stay for a few minutes."

He led me to the umbrella and insisted that I sit in the lone chair. As I settled into it, he reached into the cooler for two beers.

"I really shouldn't," I said.

He opened one and handed it to me. "Why not? It's the Fourth. Time to relax and forget all your troubles." He lowered himself to the sand and sat cross-legged. "You know, I'm really honored to be with you like this. I mean, who would have guessed a normal guy like me would be lucky enough to share a beer with the most beautiful and talented singer on the planet?"

"Oh, please," I said with a dismissive laugh. "I'm just a plain old beach girl. Everything else is makeup and the magic of the recording studio. You ought to hear me sing in the shower if you want to know how terrible I really sound."

Crap, I thought. *Why did I say that? It sounded like I was inviting him to see me in the shower, which meant I was inviting him to see me naked, which meant—*

"Anyway, I'd like to make a toast," he said, holding his bottle up. "Here's to chance meetings. We've certainly had our share of them."

I tapped his bottle with mine. "To chance meetings. And, yes, we certainly *have* had our share of them." After we both took a sip, I said, "I want to thank you again for stopping to change our tire. That was very kind of you."

"Well, you have to understand I grew up in Alabama," he said, mimicking an exaggerated southern drawl. "In my little town, we all helped each other out. So when I see someone in need, my first impulse is to assist them."

"Nice impulse to have," I said. "So did you go to college in Alabama?"

He smiled. "Auburn. But I went to med school here at the Medical University. That's my parents fault—they took me to Charleston one summer when I was a teen. I fell in love with it and knew this is where I wanted to live." He took another sip, smacked his lips, and said, "So what about you? Did you ever get a chance to go to college?"

"No," I replied with a sigh. "Not yet."

He looked at me curiously.

"I'm determined to go one day," I explained, batting away the hair that was blowing into my face. "No one in my family ever went, and I've always wanted to be the first. But it's been impossible with my crazy life. I'm hoping I can do it when I retire from music...whenever that'll be."

Our conversation drifted from subject to subject, breezy and loose. When it came time for him to ask me if I wanted another Corona, I found it easy to say yes, just so I'd have an excuse to spend more time with him.

"Can I ask you something, Dr, Drew?" I said as he opened the cap for me.

"Of course. Ask away. And please drop the doctor thing... from now on it's just Drew."

"Okay, Drew." Saying it raised the corner of my lips into a grin. "I was just wondering about something. Didn't you say yesterday at Bert's that you were having a party today?" I gestured around us. "I'm sorry, but this doesn't seem like much of a party to me. Did something happen to change your plans?"

He looked embarrassed. "Afraid so. Everyone bailed on me. It started with my brother and his wife...they decided they'd rather take their boat out than spend the day on the beach. Then one of my buddies—he's a doctor too—got called in for an emergency. And my other so-called friends came up with an assortment of excuses why they couldn't make it. So that's why I've been sitting here twiddling my thumbs—until you came along, that is."

I thought about asking him, "So, why isn't your girlfriend here?" just to see what he would say. Not that I was curious about his relationship status or anything.

Okay, maybe I was a *little* curious. After all, I wanted to make sure there wasn't someone else—just in case.

We chatted and drank a while longer. Then I happened to glance at my watch.

"Oh, gosh, I've got to go," I said, rising to my feet. "I didn't realize how long I've been here."

"What's the hurry?" He stood and wiped the sand off his trunks. "It's not like you have to be somewhere."

"I'm afraid Sara and Suzanne will get worried if I don't get back," I said.

"Call them and tell them you met this irresistibly charming man you want to spend more time with," he suggested with a chuckle.

Actually, it was true: he *was* charming and I *did* want to spend more time with him. But something—I don't know what—was telling me I'd better go.

"I don't have my phone with me," I told him.

"You can use mine," he suggested. "It's in the house." He nodded to the bungalow behind us. "I'm not on call today so I left it inside."

The bungalow didn't strike me as something a doctor would buy. It looked too run-down and in need of repair. Definitely a fixer-upper.

"Thanks for the offer," I said, "but I really have to go."

I was about to tell him goodbye when my bladder sent an urgent message to my brain: *Empty me first or you're going to leave a puddle somewhere on the beach before you make it home!*

"Is something wrong?" Drew asked.

I bit my lower lip. "Um, I was wondering...do you think I could use your bathroom? The beer—it's sorta..."

"Say no more," he interrupted with a grin. "I would be honored to have you use it."

I followed him to the bungalow, which looked like it could fall apart with the slightest breeze.

"It ain't much," Drew said (the understatement of the year), "but I got it dirt cheap. I'm planning on renovating it soon, maybe even adding a second floor. I'm kind of a hands-on guy, so I want to do some of the work myself. I probably would have taken up carpentry if I hadn't become a doctor."

"Well, I sorta like it," I said. "It's got a certain charm. Elegantly shabby, I believe they call it." Actually, there was nothing elegant about it, but I was trying to be nice.

We went inside, and I was immediately turned off by the smell of stale cigarette smoke.

As if he could read my mind, Drew said, "I know, I know, it smells like a bar in here, doesn't it? Guess the previous owner must have been a chain smoker. I'm hoping a fresh coat of paint on the walls and some new curtains will take care of the problem." He pointed to a narrow hall off the living room. "Anyway, the bathroom is that way. Just promise me you won't count how many rings are around the toilet. I'm a bachelor, you know."

Hearing that made me want to turn around and leave. But I had to go sooo bad.

Plus, I was curious to see what his living conditions were like. After all, if he was a total slob it would be good to find that out now instead of later.

But overall the house was pretty clean. Dishes were stacked neatly in the sink. The floors were swept and I saw no signs of dust. And the toilet didn't have a single ring—in fact, it appeared to have been recently scrubbed. There was even one of those tidy bowl thingys in it.

Only one problem—the confounded thing refused to flush.

"You okay in there?" Drew asked from the other side of the door.

How did he know I was having trouble?

"I'm fine," I called back. "But there's something wrong with the toilet." How embarrassing.

"You have to hold the lever down for at least ten seconds," his muffled voice instructed me. "It's kind of quirky."

I did as he said and it worked.

"Thanks," I said when I opened the door. "I was afraid I broke it."

He laughed. "There's not much around here that's not already broke. This house is pretty old—built in the forties I believe. But at least the structure is strong. From what I understand, it went through Hurricane Hugo without much damage."

Hugo. The name caused my stomach to lurch.

"Did I say something wrong?" Drew asked.

Actually, he had. But there was no way for him to know that.

"I'm sorry," I said. "It's just that—" I struggled to find the right words. "I...I have this problem. But I'll be okay."

He placed a hand on my shoulder. "You don't look okay. I think you should sit down for a few minutes."

"No, really, I'm fine."

It was a lie. I was about to break out in a cold sweat.

"I'm a doctor and I'm ordering you to rest for a few minutes." He led me to a sofa in the living room. "Let me get you a glass of water or something."

I lowered myself to the lumpy sofa; it looked like it was past due for a trip to the Salvation Army. "I don't need anything. I'm okay," I insisted.

He sat beside me. "A.J., I work with patients all day long. I can tell when something's bothering them, and right now there is definitely something bothering you. Why don't you tell me what it is?"

I nodded and offered him a weak smile. "Okay. Have you ever heard of something called Post Traumatic Stress Disorder?"

"Of course. I studied it in Medical School."

"Well, I have it. In fact, I've had it for a long time—since I was seventeen."

"*Seventeen?*" He looked surprised. "My God, what happened to you at such a young age?"

"I can't believe you don't know. I mean, you said you're a fan of mine and all...I thought everybody knew what Hugo did to me."

"It's true that I love your music. But I'm afraid I don't know much about your personal life, except that you recently got divorced."

I reminded myself that he was a doctor; he had better things to do than to catch up on my bio.

"Well, something happened to me a long time ago that left me with a big-time emotional scar," I began. "It happened right here on Folly, back in 1989. I was a senior in high school and was living out here with my family in a house my dad inherited from my grandfather. Dad thought it was built so well that it could withstand anything, including a hurricane. So when Hugo threatened the coast, he didn't evacuate. He made all of us stay right here on the beach."

"Good God, was he insane?" Drew said.

I shook my head. "No, my dad was far from insane. He was actually quite smart. But he had a stubborn streak a mile long. Once he decided something, that was it, even if you could prove him wrong. So once he decided we were going to stay, there was nothing any of us could do to convince him otherwise."

"Why didn't you just leave? Couldn't you have stayed with a friend or something?"

"Suzanne was living in downtown Charleston at the time. She invited me to stay with her, but I didn't do it. I felt too guilty leaving everyone at the beach. I figured if they were going to die, I was going to die too."

"So what happened? It must have been terrifying staying out here in a category four storm."

I took a deep breath to steady myself. This was going to be the hard part; the part that always made me cry. "It was horrible. The house shook on its pilings all night and the ocean rose so high that water seeped in through the doors. Then the eye came along with the storm surge. That was it. The waves beat the house right off its pilings. It fell apart. My parents and siblings were crushed by the second floor collapsing on top of them." Tears streaked down my cheeks. "Just before it happened, I ran to another part of the house. Somehow, I got thrown into the surf. I almost drowned, but the current took me to a roof that had blown off another house. I clung to it until the Coast Guard found me the next day. I was at the hospital when they told me my family was…gone."

Drew wiped my tears away with his thumb. "You poor thing," he whispered. "No wonder you were traumatized."

"I'm sorry to lay all this on you," I said with a sniffle. "This is the Fourth…you should be having fun instead of listening to my problems."

He slid his arm behind me. "It's okay," he said gently. "I'm glad I'm getting to know you like this. I want you to feel like you can tell me anything."

I did feel like I could tell him anything. He seemed so understanding, so compassionate. And I was falling for him. No doubt about it, I was falling for him.

"So the house you're staying in now," he continued, "is it where your old one used to be?"

I nodded. "I built it after my first song went multi-platinum. I wanted it to look as much like the old house as possible. That way it feels like I'm really coming home when I walk inside."

Drew was silent for a moment. Then he said, "You know, you're a very special lady. And I think there's a reason you survived that storm. God wanted you to. He knew the joy you were going to bring people with your music."

I wiped another tear from my cheek and thanked him for saying something so kind.

"Here, why don't you take off those sunglasses so you can dry your eyes," Drew said. He reached for them, but I jerked away.

"What's wrong?" he asked.

"It's my eye...I don't want you to see it like this."

His forehead crinkled. "Like what?"

"My daughter. She accidently hit me this morning. Now it's all black and blue."

His lips formed a crooked grin. "You keep forgetting that I'm a doctor. I'm sure I've seen a lot worse. So let me have a peek—maybe I can do something to help the swelling."

I slowly removed the shades.

Drew let out a long whistle. "Wow. You do have one heck of shiner there. Sara must throw a mean right hook."

"She's learning karate," I said. "Maybe that's why she hit me so hard. But it was just an accident. She was having a nightmare and I happened to be in the wrong place at the wrong time."

His hand brushed against my shoulder. "Well, I think you're beautiful, black eye and all. And your good eye is the loveliest shade of blue I've ever seen." He reached for my floppy hat and took it off my head. "And just look at all that gorgeous blonde hair you're hiding."

I'd been so caught up in telling him about my life that I didn't realize how close he was sitting next to me—and that he was barely dressed, with just swim trunks on.

Suddenly, I felt uncomfortable. But it was a good kind of uncomfortable; the kind of uncomfortable I used to feel around Randy, just before we'd—

"I've got to go," I said, rising to my feet.

"Wow, you decided that awfully quick," Drew said with a laugh.

"I'm sorry, but I..."

"Was feeling the same thing I was?" he offered.

I feigned surprise, even though I knew exactly what he was talking about. "Wha...what do you mean?"

His eyes sparkled mischievously. "Well, I wanted to kiss you. And I had a feeling you wanted to kiss me. So was I right, or am I getting rusty at this sort of thing?"

I stood there like a dummy, not knowing what to say.

"Can I take your silence as a yes?" he asked.

"Drew, I...I have to know something, and you have to be one hundred percent honest with me, okay?"

"One hundred percent. I promise."

I pressed my lips together, then said, "Are you truly single? I mean, there's not a girlfriend out there that you're not telling me about, right? 'Cause I know how men are. I lived with a guy who thought it was okay to cheat on me; that it didn't count because the other girls were just..."

"Go on," He prompted me with a curious grin.

"Well, to quote him, they were just a piece of ass. I don't want to be just a piece of...well, you know what. So if that's what you're after, let's just say goodbye right now."

He put his hand to his chin and rubbed it. "Well, I have to admit that your ass is pretty dogone nice. But I just so happen to like everything else that comes along with it." He stood and looked me in the eye. "A.J., you're a beautiful, talented, woman. And I'm not you're ex-husband. I would never cheat on someone as wonderful as you. I think he must have done too many drugs in his past to do something that stupid."

"He never used drugs," I said in Randy's defense. "Except for a little pot now and then. But I made him stop that."

Drew rolled his eyes. "Okay, he was just an idiot, then. But whatever the reason, he was a fool to betray you. I can promise you that I'll never do that." He moved closer. "So can I kiss you now?"

It would have better if he'd just done it and not asked. I mean, this was just plain awkward. What was I supposed to do? Pucker up?

"Drew, maybe we should wait..."

He took me in his arms and silenced me with a long, delicious kiss.

"I want to take you on a date," he whispered when we came up for air. "Tonight. How about dinner at the Starfish Grille? It's on the pier, so we can catch the fireworks show after we eat."

"Can't," I sighed. "I promised Sara I'd watch the fireworks with her and Alex."

"Invite them to join us," he suggested.

Poor guy. He didn't have a clue how awful that would turn out. I could see Sara making a disaster out of the whole thing, just so he'd never want to see me again.

"Sara's not too keen on me dating just yet," I explained. "She's having some trouble adjusting to me being single, I'm afraid."

He rubbed my back and shoulders. God, did it ever felt good. "Well, why don't we do this," he said. "You and I can have dinner together, just the two of us. Then Sara and Alex can meet up with us afterwards and we can watch the fireworks together. How's that sound?"

I was still unsure how Sara would act around him. But I couldn't pass up the opportunity to spend the evening with him, so I said, "Okay. I guess we could try that."

"I'll pick you up at seven." He kissed my cheek, then went over to the counter that separated the kitchen from the living room. "Give me your address," he said, opening up a pocket-sized notebook.

After writing it down, he came back and gave me a kiss goodbye.

A kiss that held the promise of more to come.

chapter 14

SARA WAS WAITING for me on the screen porch when I got back, hands on hips.

"Where have you been?" she demanded. "We were getting worried about you."

"I took a walk," I explained, thinking how strange it was for her to be grilling me instead of the other way around.

"Mom, you *never* take walks that long," she said. "So where were you?"

Busted, I thought. *Might as well come clean.*

I gestured toward the wicker loveseat and suggested we sit down. After we settled into the cushions, I took a deep breath, silently asked God to give me strength, and began my confession.

"You know that guy who changed the tire for us on the way here?" I said, trying to be nonchalant. "Well, you'll never guess what happened."

Sara's eyes opened wide. "Oh-my-God, you mean that creepy dude? Don't tell me you were taking your walk and ran into him?"

"Well, yeah, something like that."

"Just like the way you ran onto him at Bert's, I suppose?"

I shot her a curious look. "How did you know about *that?*"

"Suzanne told me about it." She slid low in the seat and crossed her arms. "Don't you think it's weird that he keeps showing up? I mean, it's almost like he's stalking you or something."

"Oh, don't be ridiculous," I said, draping an arm around her. "It's nothing more than coincidence. He lives out here. And it's not uncommon to keep running into the same person on Folly—it's a tiny island."

She sniffed the air and made a face. "You've been drinking, haven't you? I can smell it on your breath."

I shifted my weight in the seat. "Just a couple of beers—it's no big deal. And it's not like I had to drive home, you know."

She turned her gaze to the sea. "Maybe that guy was trying to get you drunk. Maybe he thought he'd get lucky if he did."

"That's ridiculous! I would never let myself get so intoxicated that someone could take advantage of me!" Okay, maybe I did *once*, but she didn't need to know that.

"Whatever," she muttered. "So did he ask you out?"

"As a matter fact, he did. He's taking me to dinner at the Starfish Grille. It's right down the street at the—"

"I know where it is," she butt in. "So are you going to spend the night with him?"

My mouth dropped open. "Sara! Why would you ask me something like that?"

She shrugged. "Suzanne told me you needed sex. Maybe this is your chance to get some."

I made a mental note to have a little talk with Suzanne. No scratch that, I made a mental note to *strangle* Suzanne and said, "Honey, please don't listen to her. I love her to death, but she has more than just a few screws missing. You can't take anything she says seriously."

"Oh, yeah? Funny how she says the same thing about you."

I raised a brow. "Oh, she does, does she?"

Sara brought her heels up to the edge of the loveseat and hugged her knees. "Yep. She says you're just plain loony sometimes. But she says you can't help it—it's a result of going through all that trauma in your life from Hugo."

I had to admit there was some truth to what she said. Still, my 'craziness' couldn't compare to Suzanne's.

Could it?

To my amazement, Sara leaned her head on my shoulder. "I'm really not okay with you dating that guy," she said quietly, gazing out to sea. "But I guess I have to realize you're single now and you're going to want to go out with a jerk now and then."

"He's not a jerk."

"I say he is. But if you want to date him, I won't stand in the way."

"That's very big of you," I said, stroking her hair. "Just like I won't stand in the way of you dating that jerk, Alex."

She pulled away from me. "Mom! He's not a jerk!"

I smiled. "I say he is. Guess time will tell who's right and who's wrong, huh?"

"Whatever." She got up and started for the French doors. "I'm going inside. Alex is playing Halo and I want to prove to him that I can whip his butt at it."

She went inside, and I stretched out on the loveseat to watch the tide roll in. All was peaceful until Suzanne came out to the porch and sat next to me.

She held her hand up, like she wanted to give me a high five.

"What?" I asked curiously.

"Sara told me about your rendezvous with the doctor. Way to go, kiddo."

I halfheartedly slapped her hand. "It's not a big deal. We talked for a while, that's all." I conveniently omitted the part about him kissing me.

"He asked you on a date. I'd say that's a big deal," Suzanne retorted.

"Yeah—a simple dinner date, right here on the beach at the Starfish Grill."

"Which is close to his house," she said. "Which makes it really convenient in case ya'll want to go back and do you-know-what."

I did an exaggerated eye roll. "There's not going to be any you-know-what. So don't expect me to come back and fill you in on any juicy details."

Her lips scrunched up into a dubious smile. "Uh-huh. Just remember to be careful and make sure he uses protection. You can't be too careful now-a-days, you know."

"I'm not planning on going to bed with him."

"Plans can change. All it takes is a little wine at dinner to lower your defenses. And if you tell me he doesn't give you the hots, then you're a liar."

"I never said he didn't give me the—" I glared at her. "You tricked me into saying that, didn't you?"

She laughed. "It's okay to have the hots for him. Just make sure you do something about it or you'll end up frustrated."

"Okay, enough of this," I said, rising to my feet. "I need to figure out what I'm going to wear and take a shower. He'll be here before I know it—we're going to dinner early so we can meet up with you guys for the fireworks show afterwards."

She waved me off. "Forget about us and make some fireworks of your own. I'll take the kids down to the pier to see the show. You just concentrate on having a good time with the doctor. I want you to have so much fun that you'll regret what you did tomorrow."

"You're hopeless, you know that?"

I turned to go inside, but she stopped me by asking, "Hey, what are you going to do about your black eye?"

"Wear sunglasses, I guess," I said with a shrug.

"Oh, that's really romantic! Don't you want to be able to look Dr. Drew in the eye? Let me see if I can work a little magic on you with some of my theatrical makeup."

"But what if someone recognizes me and sees that I have a black eye? Next thing you know, it'll be in all the trash magazines. They'll probably say Randy beat me up or something."

"They won't know you have a black eye when I get through with you," she assured me.

I took my shower, and after I dried my hair and slipped into a strapless sundress, Suzanne came in and went to work on me, applying her 'special' makeup and twisting my hair into an elegant French braid.

"You look awesome!" she declared when she was done.

I peered into the mirror above my dresser and smiled. She had done an excellent job, better than some of the so-called professionals who were responsible for making me look good for my shows.

"Wow, I can't tell I have a black eye," I said, staring into the mirror in disbelief. "And you're quite the braider."

"Damn right, I am," she said proudly. "And you're quite the hottie. Just wait until that doctor gets a load of you. He'll need to do CPR on himself."

Sara poked her head inside the door. Her jaw went slack when she saw me.

"Holy crap, Mom, you look beautiful!" she said, grinning from ear to ear.

"You can thank Suzanne for that," I told her.

Sara looked down at the CD she was holding. "You think I can talk to you for a minute?" she asked me.

"Sure. Come on in."

She gave Suzanne a peculiar look. "Um, you think I could be alone with my mom for a minute?" she asked.

Suzanne nodded. "Sure thing, kiddo." On her way out the door, she gave Sara a wink and said, "Your mom's a total babe, ain't she?"

Sara giggled and waited for her to close the door. Then she walked across the room and handed me the unlabeled CD.

"What's this?" I asked.

"I want you to have it," she said. "I downloaded it a little while ago. I want you to listen to the lyrics."

"What song is it?"

Her eyes glistened, like she was about to cry. "Just listen to it. It's something I think you should do, but it says it better than I can."

I reached for her, but she backed away.

"Honey, why are you doing this?" I asked. "If you have something to say to me, just say it."

"I'd rather do it with the song," she insisted. "I think it's better that way."

"Do you want me to put it on now?" I asked.

"No, do it after I leave."

"Okay, but are you sure you don't want to talk about this? You look upset."

She hurried to the door. With her back turned to me, she said, "I hope you have a good time tonight—even though I think you're making a big mistake."

"Sara, I don't—"

Before I could finish, she slipped out the door.

With a heavy sigh, I took my laptop from its case and powered it up. When it finished booting, I inserted the CD and turned up the volume.

A haunting piano solo filled the room. I instantly recognized it as the beginning to DHT's 'Listen to Your Heart.'

"Nice try, Sara," I whispered to myself, knowing this was her way of asking me to give her dad another chance. "But it's not going to work. I'm over him now—time to move on with my life."

I went to the dresser and picked up a bottle of Channel No. 5.

I dabbed a little on my neck.

And some between my breasts...

Just in case.

chapter 15

IT WAS THREE AM when I got back to the house.

I didn't plan on getting home that late, but then again I didn't plan on falling asleep in a strange bed, either.

It all began with a pleasant dinner with Drew. We talked, we laughed, we flirted, and before desert was served, we were holding hands.

Then we took a stroll along the pier, where we met up with Sara, Suzanne, and Alex. Drew went out of his way to be nice to Sara, but she snubbed him and asked me if she could go with Alex to the west end of the beach. "It's where they're going to launch the fireworks," she said. "It'll be awesome, Mom...I heard someone say you're so close you can feel the heat from the rockets when they explode. Please let us go!"

At first I said no, but she pestered me so much that I finally gave in. "I'll let you do it, but you have to promise me two things," I told her. "First, you don't leave Alex's side. Second, I want you home as soon as the show is over. No dawdling."

She let me know she was 'down with that' and hurried off. Then it was Suzanne's turn to abandon us.

"I'm not into fireworks," she explained. "I think I'd rather do some bar-crawling on Center Street. Ya'll want to join me?"

Drew and I told her no thanks and made our way to the end of the pier, where he stood behind me with his arms wrapped around my waist during the show. After the grand finale, he kissed me on the cheek and suggested we go back to his house for a drink.

One thing led to another. Next thing I knew I woke up in his bed, exhausted yet fulfilled from hours of lovemaking.

That was around two A.M. I wanted to leave, but Drew asked me to stay until morning.

"I can't do that. It wouldn't set a good example for Sara," I let him know.

Drew said he understood, but began kissing me along my neck. His fingers traced a line up my inner thigh until they found...

That's why I didn't make it home until three.

Luckily, I found the house quiet and still.

Good, everyone's asleep, I thought. *Maybe they'll never know I got back this late.*

I considered sneaking up to Sara's room to make sure she was okay—and alone. After all, there was no telling what kind of shenanigans her and Alex might get into without me around to chaperone them. But the stairs were so squeaky that I was afraid I might wake her. So I tippy-toed to the downstairs guest room instead.

I cracked the door open and found Alex curled under the covers, snoring.

Everything's okay, I thought. *Now I can sleep in peace.*

It was an assumption I would regret for the rest of my life.

chapter 16

I WOKE TO the sound of thunder.

It rattled the walls of the house. Then came the pitter-patter of rain on the roof.

I rolled onto my side and pulled the covers over my head. I hated thunder; it reminded me of Hugo and that awful night when...

"A.J.?"

It was Suzanne's voice. I could tell by the sound of it that something was wrong.

I pulled the covers down and squinted at the doorway where she stood. Her hair was messy, pulled into a loose bun. A pair of thick-lens glasses sat halfway down her nose, a sign that she hadn't put her contacts in yet. And she clutched nervously at the sides of her pink cotton robe.

I sat up and asked her what was the matter.

"I think you should come into the living room," she replied with a shaken voice.

"Why?" I asked, feeling my body grow tense.

A lone tear cascaded down her cheek. "You need to talk to Alex," she said. "It's about Sara."

My heart rate doubled as I swung my legs to the floor, slipped into a robe, and rushed past her into the living room.

I found Alex sitting on the sofa with his head cradled in his hands. "I'm so sorry, Ms. Jenkins," he said, avoiding my gaze. "I didn't mean for this to happen."

A cold fear caught in my throat, making it difficult to speak. But I managed to ask, "What are you talking about? Where's Sara?"

He shook his head and began to weep. "She's gone, Ms. Jenkins. I don't know where she is."

"What do you mean, *she's gone?*"

Alex stood. Suzanne came up behind me and placed a hand on my shoulder.

"Please don't be mad at me, Ms. Jenkins," he sobbed. "I know you told me to keep my eye on her, but something happened."

Fear gave way to anger. "What the hell are you talking about, Alex?" I snapped. "Where's my daughter?"

"A.J., try to stay calm and let him explain," Suzanne said.

Alex lowered his gaze to the floor. "You know how we went down to the west end of the beach to watch the fireworks show? Well, when it was over we sat on the blanket we carried down there and talked for a while—I swear, Ms. Jenkins, that's all we were doing."

"Get to the point!" I cried.

He sniffled and continued, "Well, we were both pretty tired, especially Sara, so we laid down on the blanket—you know, just to rest. We were looking up at the stars and trying to find some of the constellations—Sara likes stuff like that—and I was pointing some of them out to her when I noticed she was drifting off to sleep. So I figured I'd let her take a little nap. But then I fell asleep too. I must have been really tired, Ms. Jenkins, 'cause I didn't wake up until a couple of hours later. She was gone, so I came back here and—"

I didn't let him finish. Instead, I bolted upstairs and threw the door to Sara's room open.

Her bed was unmade. Several shirts and shorts were laid out on it.

"Ms. Jenkins, she's not there," Alex called out from downstairs. "That's what I've been trying to tell you." I heard his footsteps as he climbed the staircase. When he reached me, I was still staring at Sara's bed, as if in a daze.

I heard him say, "I thought she came back home, Ms. Jenkins. I thought she left me sleeping on the blanket and went home to get in her bed. I didn't realize she wasn't here until this morning. I came up to see if she wanted to sit on the porch and watch the rain with me—she likes the rain, you know—but I saw she wasn't here. That's when I knew something was wrong and woke up Suzanne."

"She hasn't been home," Suzanne said, coming up behind me. "I know it for a fact. Her clothes are lying on the bed in the exact same spot they were in when I was helping her decide what to wear to the fireworks show last night." Her lone tear was joined by others now. "She never made it home, A.J. This is serious...really serious."

I raced down the stairs and into my room. Suzanne and Alex followed.

"What are you doing?" Suzanne asked, watching me jerk the covers from my bed.

"Maybe she decided to sleep in here," I said. "She scared me like this once before."

"She's not in your bed, A.J.," Suzanne said solemnly.

I stopped and looked at the empty mattress. "Maybe she's hiding somewhere else. Did you check your bed?"

"She's not in my bed," Suzanne said, moving closer to me. "She's not here, honey."

"No, she has to be!" I insisted. "We just have to find her!" I ran into the living room and called out her name.

"A.J., we have to call the police," Suzanne said.

"No! She's not missing! I'll find her!"

She followed me to the porch. I opened the screen door and ran out to the beach.

It was pouring rain, but I didn't care. I had to find Sara.

"A.J., stop!" Suzanne cried. She was right behind me when I reached the edge of the sea.

"You go the left and I'll go to the right," I said, blinking the rain out of my eyes. "We'll keep walking until one of us finds her."

She grabbed me by the shoulders. "A.J., listen to me! The police can canvass the beach a lot quicker than we can. We need to go inside and call them. Every minute counts right now."

The rain came down harder. I fell to my knees and dug my fingers into the wet sand. "No!" I cried. "This can't be happening! This just can't be happening!"

Suzanne knelt beside me, the lenses of her eyeglasses dotted with rain drops. "You've got to get a grip, honey. I know how upset you are, but freaking out like this isn't going to help anything. You've got to be strong for Sara."

I shook all over. "You think someone got her? You think whoever took those other girls has her?"

"I don't know. But we have to call the police." She stood and offered to help me up.

"This is all my fault," I said, taking her hand. "I should have checked on her last night when I came home. I shouldn't have gone on that date. I should have stayed home."

She hooked her arm in mine and walked me back to the house. "Blaming yourself isn't going to solve anything," she said. "You need to stay focused. The police are going to ask a million questions. You have to be ready to answer them."

Alex was waiting for us on the screen porch. "Are you going to call the cops?" he asked.

Something inside me snapped.

"You little bastard!" I shouted, lurching for him. "I told you not to let Sara out of your sight!"

"A.J., stop!" Suzanne cried.

I took him by the shoulders and shook him. "If I find out you had anything to do with this, I swear I'll kill you! You hear me? I'll kill you!"

"For Christ's sake stop!" Suzanne yelled. "Can't you tell he's as worried as we are?"

I let go of him. He wiped the tears from his shocked face with the back of his hand and ran inside the house.

"Jesus, what's wrong with you?" Suzanne asked. She made me sit on the wicker loveseat. "Now take some deep breaths and try to calm your ass down while I get my phone."

I fell into such a deep daze that I didn't know she had returned until I heard her ask, "Do you want to do this?"

She was holding a cell phone out for me to take.

I shook my head. "I...I can't."

She nodded. "Okay, I'll do it, then."

She punched in 9-1-1 and brought the phone to her ear.

Seconds later, she spoke the words that no mother wants to hear:

"I need to report a missing teenager."

chapter 17

"GOOD MORNING, MA'AM, I'm Officer Steve Bradley with the Folly Beach Police. I was sent here to take a missing per...." The young man's words trailed off and the color drained from his face.

"Are you okay?" Suzanne asked. She opened the door wider and gestured for him to come inside.

The officer stared at her, open mouthed. "Did anyone ever tell you that you look like Suzanne Richardson?" he asked.

"I *am* Suzanne Richardson," she said. "But this is no time for you to get star struck. So get your ass in here and help us find Sara."

The officer, who looked fresh out of college, stepped across the threshold. His eyes became saucers when he saw me sitting at the dining room table. "Holy crap, you're...you're A.J., aren't you?" he stuttered. "The famous singer, right?"

I clasped my trembling hands in my lap to still them and nodded.

"Wow, I can't believe this," he said, making his way to the table. "My wife is going to flip when she finds out I've met you. She loves all your songs—especially the new one you have out."

"Okay, this isn't a freakin' fan club meeting," Suzanne butted in. "Her daughter is missing and we're worried sick over what's happened to her. So why don't you get down to business and stop all the bullshit."

"Sorry," the officer said with an apologetic smile. "It's just that I wasn't expecting to come face to face with two celebrities. Nothing like this has ever happened in my six months on the force."

"Oh, great," Suzanne groaned. "A rookie—just what we need." She stood behind my chair and added, "Why don't you call your chief or somebody who actually has some experience. This is serious shit."

The officer paid no attention to her and asked me if it was okay for him to sit down. I told him yes, and he pulled out the chair across from me. "I'd like to begin by asking you a few questions, A.J.," he said.

"It's Ms. Jenkins to you," Suzanne corrected him.

"Sorry. Do you mind if I ask you a few questions, Ms. Jenkins?"

I heard his words, but I didn't respond. Everything—the officer, the room, Suzanne—seemed distant. It was a familiar feeling; the same one I'd experienced after learning my family had perished during Hurricane Hugo.

"Ms. Jenkins? Are you okay?" Officer Bradley asked.

"Of course, she's not okay," Suzanne answered for me. "She's scared to death. What mother wouldn't be in a situation like this?"

"I understand," Officer Bradley said. "But I really need to ask her a few questions."

"Then ask me," I said, my voice sounding as distant as everything else.

He opened a notepad and took a pen from his shirt pocket. "Can you tell me the last time you saw your daughter?"

"Last night, just before the fireworks show," I said. "She went with her boyfriend to the west end of the beach to see them up close."

"What time was that?" he asked.

"I guess around nine...maybe a little later."

"And when did you realize she was missing?"

"This morning. When Alex told me."

Officer Bradley looked up from his pad. "Alex? Who's Alex?"

"Her boyfriend," Suzanne replied.

He looked puzzled. "So Alex came back but Sara didn't?"

Suzanne told him about Alex falling asleep and waking up to find her gone.

"So Alex is here, staying with you?" Officer Bradley asked me.

I nodded.

"Where is he now?"

"In his guest room," I said. "Maybe you should go in there and talk to him. I've got a feeling he's not telling us everything."

"Why's that?"

"Intuition, I suppose. I can't shake the feeling he's lying about something."

Officer Bradley nodded. "We'll do a thorough interview with the boy. If there's a hole in his story, I'm sure we'll discover it."

Suzanne spoke up. "That's all well and good, but what are you going to do to *find* Sara? Shouldn't you be doing one of those Amber Alerts?"

"I'm going to send out a BOLO as soon as I get her description," he said. Turning his dark eyes to me, he asked, "Do you have a recent photo of Sara?"

"I have one in my purse," I told him.

Suzanne volunteered to get it for me. While she was gone, I found myself staring at the patch on Officer Bradley's shoulder. It was the official logo for Folly Beach, which included a starfish, a sand dollar, and two stalks of sea oats. The sand dollar reminded me of Sara and how much she loved to collect them.

I burst into tears.

"Can I get you a tissue, Ms. Jenkins?" Officer Bradley offered.

"I have some with me," Suzanne said, returning to the room. "I figured she was going to need them." She handed me two tissues and gave Officer Bradley the photo of Sara.

He studied it for a moment. Then he asked me how tall she was, how much she weighed, and what she was wearing when she went missing. He jotted it all down on his notepad, then he unclipped the walkie-talkie from his belt and relayed the information to his dispatcher. "Send a BOLO out immediately," he told her. "And please have Chief Bowers come to my location."

"Are you sure about that?" the dispatcher asked. Her voice sounded grumpy through the walkie-talkie's tiny speaker.

Officer Bradley looked annoyed. "Yes, I'm sure about that. I need him to come here as soon as possible. This is a special case."

"But it's his day off," the dispatcher said. "He's probably playing golf. He's going to be pissed unless this is really urgent."

Officer Bradley grimaced as he keyed the mic. "Grace, I wouldn't ask for him unless it's important! This is a priority situation. The missing girl is a celebrity's daughter."

"Who's the celebrity?" she asked excitedly. "Is it Angelina Jolie? I heard she might be visiting Folly this month."

Through gritted teeth, Officer Bradley said, "Just do as I say and notify the chief!" He put the walkie-talkie down on the table and shook his head. "I'm sorry about that. Our dispatcher tends to be a little nosey."

"Great," Suzanne sighed. "I can't tell you how thrilled I am to have you guys handling this situation. Maybe you ought to get Goober involved too, since it looks like Andy and Barney are out playing golf."

"I assure you that our police force is as professional as any other," Officer Bradley said. "We may be a small force but we're mighty good at what we do."

"And what would that be?" Suzanne shot back. "Giving out parking tickets? That's all I ever see you guys do."

"Ms. Richardson, please, I assure you that—"

"Maybe you should turn this case over to the FBI," she interrupted. "I don't think you're equipped to handle it. Maybe you should—"

"Maybe you should shut up!" I snapped. "All your yapping is slowing things down, Suzanne, so stop bitching and let the man do his job!"

Officer Bradley gave me an appreciative nod. Suzanne laid a hand on my shoulder and said, "I'm sorry. I just want to make sure they're doing everything they can to find Sara."

"I give you my word that we will," Officer Bradley said, rising from his seat. "I'd like to talk to the boy who was with Sara now. Would you please have him come in here?"

Suzanne went to get him. When they returned, I gave Alex a dirty stare. "You better tell the officer everything you know," I warned him. "You better not hold anything back, and you better not lie."

"Yes ma'am," he said, hanging his head low.

Officer Bradley sat on the sofa with Alex and listened to him recite the same story he'd told me and Suzanne. When Alex finished, Officer Bradley asked him if he'd seen any suspicious people hanging around before he fell asleep.

"No, sir," Alex replied. "There were a few other people lying on blankets like we were, but nobody looked weird or anything." He snapped his fingers. "Oh, wait a minute...there was one strange-looking dude walking around. He was kinda old—maybe around fifty. Had a beard and long hair—hippy kinda looking dude, you know what I mean? Didn't have a shirt on, which wasn't a big deal since it was warm outside and all, but he had lot of hair on his chest." He chuckled. "He looked like Bigfoot, man. It made Sara laugh at him. Well, not *at* him, but she laughed and sorta pointed at him. I think he might have seen her do it. He kinda gave her a look—you know, one of those 'what the hell are you looking at' looks. Yeah, he was really creepy."

Officer Bradley was about to ask him another question when we heard a knock at the door.

Suzanne opened it, and a burly-looking man with salt and pepper hair wearing khaki shorts and a white golf shirt introduced himself as Chief Bowers.

He came over to the dining table where I sat and said, "Ms. Jenkins, it's a pleasure to meet you. I had a feeling you were the celebrity Grace was referring to. I've heard rumors you and Ms. Richardson were visiting the beach this week." He extended a beefy hand.

I gave it a weak shake.

He glanced at Officer Bradley. "Who's the boy?" he asked.

"The missing girl's boyfriend," he answered. "He was the last one to see her."

Chief Bowers nodded. "Keep talking to him while I ask Ms. Jenkins a few questions." He pointed to the chair across from me. "Mind if I have a seat?"

Once he got settled, he said, "I know how hard this is on you. But let me assure you that we'll do everything we can to find Sara. I've been doing this for a long time, and the good news is that in most cases everything turns out fine. Usually the teen is simply acting out or has gotten into some sort of mischief. Unfortunately, that's pretty easy to do on a beach like this."

"Oh, really?" Suzanne said sarcastically as she slid out the chair next to me and sat down. "I wonder if that's the same thing you told the parents of those girls who've been missing for a while? Guess you think they just got into a little mischief, huh?"

He narrowed his blue-gray eyes at her. "Rest assured that we'll treat this as a worst case scenario…but there's also the possibility that Sara is missing voluntarily."

"No, she's not," I said. "She wouldn't do that."

He gave me a condescending smile. "You won't believe how many parents have told me that very same thing, only to have their child show up the next day."

"Not Sara," I said.

He nodded. "Well, let's not debate that anymore. I'd like to get a metal picture of what happened before she went missing. Could you tell me everything that led up to her disappearance?"

I told him everything I knew. When I finished, he asked, "So where were you during the fireworks show?"

I averted his gaze and replied, "Here. I was here at the house."

Suzanne's eyebrows lifted into a questioning curve.

Chief Bowers must have noticed, 'cause he asked her, "Do you have something to add to this, Ms. Richardson?"

"No," she said tentatively. "I have nothing to add."

"Were you here as well?" he asked her.

She hesitated before answering. "I...I was at a couple of nightclubs. I got back around one in the morning."

Chief Bowers turned his attention to me. "Ms. Jenkins, forgive me for asking you this, but didn't you realize something was wrong last night? I mean, if I had a sixteen year-old daughter I'd be pretty concerned if she didn't come home at a reasonable hour."

"I was asleep," I lied. "I was tired. I went to bed early. That's why I didn't know anything was wrong until this morning."

He rubbed his forehead. "I see. Then let me ask you this—have you experienced any problems with Sara lately? Anything that would make her want to run away?"

"I already told you she wouldn't do something like that. Sara faces her problems head-on. She doesn't run from them."

"So were there problems? Have you two been in any arguments recently? Any fights?"

I looked down at my hands. "No."

"Tell me, Ms. Jenkins, does Sara have violent tendencies?"

I jerked my head up. "Why would you ask me such a thing?"

"Yeah, why would you ask her such a thing?" Suzanne echoed. "Sara's a good kid, not some thug. And don't you think you'd be more productive if you got off your butt and actually did something to find her instead of grilling A.J. like this?"

The look Chief Bowers gave her was menacing. "Ms. Richardson, it would behoove you to keep your comments to yourself and show some respect. This isn't a Hollywood set. We don't solve problems in a half-hour like they do in your movies. So if you don't mind..." He turned to me and said, "The reason I asked you that, Ms. Jenkins, is because you have a pretty good shiner. Would you care to explain how that happened?"

I instinctively raised my hand to my eye. "It was an accident," I explained. "Sara was sleeping with me and had a bad dream. She lashed out and hit me."

"But you just said she wasn't violent. Doesn't that seem like a contradiction?"

"It was a freakin' dream!" Suzanne exploded. "I bet you get hard-ons in your sleep. That doesn't mean you're a freaking rapist, now does it?"

Chief Bowers face flushed a deep red. He pointed a finger at Suzanne and said, "One more outburst, Ms. Richardson, and I'll have you arrested for interfering with an investigation."

She gave him a dismissive wave of her hand. "Yeah, right, I'd like to see you try it."

He stood and asked Officer Bradley for his cuffs.

"Oh, for Christ's sake, cool your jets," Suzanne said. "I'm just looking out for A.J., that's all."

"So am I," he said. "And for the missing girl. So if you'd like me to do my job you'll stop interrupting me."

He sat back down and took a deep breath. "Ms. Jenkins, I'm simply trying to rule out the possibility that you two had a fight and that's why Sara ran away. Please forgive me if I'm upsetting you."

"She didn't run away," I said adamantly. "How many times do I have to tell you that? Whoever has those other girls took her. I just know it."

"How can you be so sure?"

"I saw the poster with the girls' pictures on it. They look a lot like Sara. I think whoever's doing this has a thing for girls with blonde hair and blue eyes."

"You're assuming they've been abducted. That hasn't been proved yet."

"You've got to be kidding!" Suzanne snorted. "What do you *think* happened? Aliens abducted them while they were walking on the beach? It's foul play, Sherlock, plain and simple."

To my surprise, Chief Bowers kept his cool. "There's no evidence of foul play in those cases. We don't even know at this point if those two cases are related. And I'm certainly not going to jump to conclusions and lump Sara's case in with theirs." He swiveled in his chair to face Officer Bradley. "I want you to take a look around the house, inside and out, while I interview the boy."

"But I just told the officer everything that happened," Alex protested. "Why do you need me to tell it to you too?"

Chief Bower's answer was simple and direct: "Because I'm the chief."

Alex's lips formed an "Oh."

The chief stood. "Did Sara bring a computer with her?" he asked me.

"A laptop," I said. "It should be up in her room."

He nodded. "I'd like to take it back to the station. Sometimes kids get involved with unsavory types online. I'd like to see who she's been emailing and chatting with."

"Only Alex as far as I know," I said. "But take it if you think it will help."

"Does she have a cell phone? Did she happen to have it with her last night?" he asked.

"I made her leave it in Malibu," I said, realizing now what a big mistake that had been. If she had it with her last night she might have been able to call for help.

Chief Bowers lowered his voice and said, "I'm going to talk to the boy now. After that I'm going to have him take me to the exact spot on the beach where they were last night." He frowned and added, "However, I'm afraid the rain we had this morning has probably washed away any clues that might help us."

"Just find her," I said, giving him a pleading look. "I don't care what you have to do. I can give you money if it helps. Just find my baby. Please find my baby."

"We'll do everything we can, Ms. Jenkins. I give you my word."

He went to talk to Alex, and while he did, Officer Bradley had me take him to Sara's room. "I just want to make sure nothing looks unusual," he explained. "I hope you understand."

"I don't mind," I told him. "But I don't see how this is going to help if she never came back home."

After he took a good look around the room, Officer Bradley gathered Sara's laptop and IPod. "Did she have any other electronic devices?" he asked me.

"Just a MyFi," I told him. "Suzanne gave it to her as a present. I don't see it anywhere, so she must have taken it with her."

When he was done, he excused himself and said he was going to take a look around outside. That's when Suzanne took me by the arm and led me downstairs to the screen porch.

She closed the French doors so Chief Bowers and Alex couldn't hear her and said, "You know what you have to do now, don't you?"

I shook my head.

"You need to call Randy, that's what. He's Sara's father, A.J. He has a right to know what's going on."

"No," I said, covering my face with my hands. "I can't. He's going to hate me. He told me all along that it was too dangerous for me and Sara to come here without some sort of security."

"Regardless, you have to tell him," she said.

"You do it. I can't talk to him."

"No way. This needs to come from you." She handed me her cell phone.

"I'll break down," I said. "I can't do it without crying."

"Then cry. But tell him he needs to come here. We need all the help we can get, especially with the Mayberry cops running the show."

I punched in his number. My hands trembled as I raised the phone to my lips.

"Hey, Suzanne," Randy answered in a groggy voice. "Haven't heard from you in a while. But did you have to call me so damn early?"

I couldn't force any words out.

"Suzanne? What's wrong?"

"It's not Suzanne," I managed to say.

"A.J.? Is that you? Why does the caller ID say it's Suzanne?"

"I'm using her phone," I said, my voice cracking and unsteady.

"What's wrong? It sounds like you're crying."

"It's Sara," I sobbed. "Something bad has happened to her." My chest heaved and I felt nauseous.

"Oh, my God, has she been in an accident?" he asked.

"No. We don't know where she is. She's gone, Randy."

"*Gone?* What the hell do you mean, she's gone?"

"I think someone got her. I'm so scared...I don't know what to do."

"Dammit, A.J.! I told you not to go to that beach without a bodyguard, didn't I? But you never listen to a thing I tell you. You always think you can make up the rules as you go along."

"I just wanted to be alone with her," I said. "That's all I wanted—some time alone with my daughter."

"I can't believe you would let something like this happen. Why didn't you watch her better?"

Suzanne grabbed the phone from me and yelled into it, "Listen, you asshole, stop blaming her for this and get your butt on a flight down here! She needs you to comfort her, not lay a guilt trip on her! So you better leave your stinking attitude in L.A., you hear me?"

There was a short pause, then I heard him say, "I'm sorry. I'm just in shock over this. I'll get there as fast as possible. Can I talk to A.J.?"

I shook my head.

"She's too upset to talk," Suzanne told him. "So get your ass down here." She clicked the phone off.

At that same moment Officer Bradley climbed the steps to the porch.

"Didn't Alex say he took a blanket for him and Sara to sit on last night?" he asked me from the other side of the screen door.

"I think so," I said, wiping the tears from my cheeks.

He pursed his lips and nodded. "I need to see the chief, then. I found a blanket lying on the ground out here. It's got something on it that he's definitely going to want to take a look at."

chapter 18

THAT NIGHT I placed a candle in the window facing the ocean in Sara's room.

"I'm going to do this every night until she comes home," I told Suzanne as I held a match to it. The flame flickered and danced, then settled into a steady glow.

"I can't believe Sara is really missing," she said as she sat on the edge of the bed. "It just doesn't seem real. And that thing about the blanket..." Her voice trailed off.

My eyes remained fixed on the flame. "Didn't I tell you Alex was hiding something?"

"Maybe...but I know he wouldn't hurt Sara," she said. "There has to be another explanation for the drops of blood they found on the blanket."

"Well, if you ask me they should take him to jail and lock him up. I don't believe him for one minute when he says he doesn't know how it got there." I crossed the room and sat down beside her. "All I know is his dad better get here quick and get him out of my sight."

We were silent for a few moments, lost in our thoughts while we stared blankly at the flame.

"It's getting late," Suzanne said with a yawn. "Why don't you try to get some rest?"

"I can't. Everytime I close my eyes I imagine all the horrible things that could happen to Sara."

"Would it help if I sleep with you? I'll try not to snore."

I let my exhausted body go limp and collapsed across the bed. "If I sleep anywhere it's going to be right here. At least it'll help me feel close to Sara." I reached for her pillow, brought it to my nose, and inhaled deeply. The scent of her favorite perfume, Pacific Paradise by Escada, brought sad tears to my eyes.

Suzanne stretched out beside me and turned the lamp off, leaving the candle as the room's only light.

We lay still for a while, both of us quiet until Suzanne said, "A.J., can I ask you something?"

"Mm-hm," I murmured.

"Well, I've been waiting until we were in private to bring this up." She turned on her side to face me. "Why did you lie to Chief Bowers today? You know, about being home all night. Why didn't you tell him about your date with Dr. Drew?"

I let out a long breath. "I didn't see any point to it. If the media and paparazzi finds out about him they'll hound him to death. So I did it to protect him—and to keep the world from finding out what a terrible parent I am."

"Why would they think you're a terrible parent? You didn't do anything wrong. You thought Alex would keep Sara safe. How were you supposed to know he'd fall asleep?"

I put the pillow behind my head and closed my eyes. "I shouldn't have done it—I shouldn't have spent the night with a man I hardly knew. I should have been home, making sure Sara was okay."

Suzanne stroked my arm. "Stop beating yourself up. It's not your fault."

"Yes it is. If I'd been home I would have known she hadn't got back at a reasonable hour. I would have gone looking for her. Maybe I would have found her before..." I broke down into another crying spell.

Suzanne took me in her arms and held me close. "Hush, hush," she whispered. "It's going to be okay. Everything's going to be okay. We'll find Sara and celebrate by going shopping and getting her everything and anything she ever desired."

I laughed through my tears. "That'll cost a fortune."

"She's worth it."

"Yes, she is," I said quietly.

It took several hours, but eventually my body succumbed to fatigue and I drifted off to sleep.

It was a fitful sleep, one full of nightmares about Sara screaming and reaching out for me.

One such nightmare woke me with a start just as the sun began to rise.

"It's okay," Suzanne said. "It's just a bad dream."

I sat up and listened to something in the distance—a sound that caused my pulse to quicken.

"Do you hear it?" I asked Suzanne.

"Hear what?"

"Sirens," I said. "They're getting closer."

She raised up on her elbows. "Yeah, I hear them now. Sounds like a couple of fire engines."

I jumped out of bed and hurried downstairs to the kitchen window. The sirens grew louder as I opened the mini-blinds.

Suzanne caught up with me and wanted to know what I was doing.

"Something's going on," I told her. "Something bad."

"It's probably just a car accident," she said. "Don't get all worked up about it."

"No," I said adamantly. "It's something bad. I can feel it in my bones. It's got something to do with Sara."

She joined me at the window as I watched one fire engine whiz by, followed by another.

"See?" Suzanne said. "Someone probably burned their breakfast. So stop worrying."

A police car raced down the street, strobes flashing.

"No, there's something else going on," I said. "Something bad."

Two more police cruisers passed the house, sirens blaring.

"Don't jump to conclusions," Suzanne said. "I'm sure it has nothing to do with Sara."

"I think we ought to call Chief Bowers," I said. "Or maybe we ought to get in the car and find out where they're going."

"Let's just wait." she said. "Try to relax. You want some coffee?"

Alex startled both of us by sneaking into the kitchen and asking, "What's going on? What's with all the sirens?"

I looked at him with a steely gaze. "Why'd you creep up on us like that? You want to give us a heart attack?"

He ran his fingers through his disheveled hair. "I…I'm sorry. I guess I have quiet feet. I didn't mean to—"

"I don't give a damn what your excuse is!" I clenched my fists as a white-hot anger flared up inside me. "I just want you to come clean and tell me what *really* happened on the beach before Sara went missing. And this time, it better be the truth!"

Alex took a few steps backwards. "I already told you everything, Ms. Jenkins. Honest, I did."

"Then how did blood get on the blanket?"

"A.J., please stop," Suzanne implored me. "Yelling at Alex isn't going to help anything."

I shot her a look. "Hell no, I'm not stopping! Not until this little bastard tells me the truth!" I moved closer to him—close enough for him to feel my hot breath in his face. "You tell me, Alex," I said with my eyes narrowed. "You tell me everything right now, or you'll wish you were never born!"

He swallowed hard. "I'm not lying to you. I would never hurt Sara. I love her."

I stomped my foot. "Then how did the blood get on the blanket?"

Tears flooded his eyes. "I don't know. I didn't even know it was there. Honest, I didn't."

"Stop lying to me!"

"Okay, enough's enough," Suzanne said, pulling me away from him. "This isn't going to solve anything."

"Go back to your room," I ordered Alex. "I can't stand to see your face!"

He lowered his head and scurried off.

"God, what's gotten into you?" Suzanne asked me. "You need to get a grip."

I was about to tell her to go to hell when another siren caught my attention.

I went to the window and waited.

This time it wasn't a fire engine or a police cruiser.

It was a black van.

The words stenciled on the side if it caused my heart to sink: *Charleston County Coroner.*

I pulled away from the window and searched for my car keys.

chapter 19

"YOU'RE NOT DRIVING," Suzanne said as she followed me across the front yard toward the driveway. "You're too upset to get behind the wheel."

I realized she was probably right and tossed her the keys. "Fine, but you better drive fast!"

We got into the Jag, and as she backed it out of the driveway she said, "Okay, I'll drive fast, but would you kindly tell me *where* we're going?"

"Head toward the county park," I told her. "I've got a feeling that's where the cops were going."

We sped down the entire length of West Ashley Avenue, the main road that runs parallel to the shore, until we reached the entrance to the park. Later in the day it would be packed with beachgoers who liked the convenience of having restrooms, showers, and a snack bar nearby. But right now the parking lot was empty and a gate prevented us from going further.

"It's not even open yet," Suzanne said. "And I don't see any emergency vehicles. So now what?"

"We go down all the side streets between here and the house," I told her. "They have to be somewhere close. It shouldn't take long to find them."

I was right; the first road we turned down led us straight to the emergency vehicles. They were parked in front of a small marina on the bank of the Folly River, the brackish waterway that snakes along the lee side of the island.

After we came to a stop in the parking lot, Suzanne turned to me and said, "You see? I told you this didn't have anything to do with Sara. It's probably a boating accident."

I wasn't convinced. "I'm not leaving until I know for sure. Let's find someone who can tell us what's going on."

The words had barely left my lips when a Folly Beach officer tapped on the driver's side window.

"Morning ladies," he said as Suzanne lowered it. "We're asking people to stay away from the marina this morning. So I'm afraid I'll have to ask you to leave."

"What happened?" Suzanne asked.

The officer, who sported a close-cropped military haircut, took off his sunglasses and squinted at her. "Hey, wait a minute...don't I know you?" His forehead crumpled and he snapped his fingers. "Don't tell me, I'll get it in a minute." More finger snapping. "You're that movie star...Suzanna Richardson, right?"

"It's Suzanne not Suzanna," she corrected him. "And I'd really appreciate it if you would tell us what's going on here."

The officer turned his eyes to me. "Oh, man, this can't be happening! You're A.J., the singer, right?"

"Yes, she is," Suzanne said. "She's also the mother of the teenage girl who went missing yesterday, so you can imagine how upsetting it is for her to see all these emergency vehicles and not know what's going on."

The officer looked around the parking lot nervously, then lowered his voice and said, "All I can tell you is they found a floater. That's police jargon for a drowning victim."

"I know what a floater is," Suzanne said. I could tell she was straining to be polite. "Is there anything else you can tell us?"

"Not really, ma'am. I'm just out here to keep people from getting too close to the investigation team. If you want to know more, you'll have to speak to Chief Bowers. He's in charge."

"Well, could you be a sweetie and go get him for us?" Suzanne asked.

He smiled. "You know, you're even more beautiful in person than you are in the movies, even without all that makeup on. And I thought you were awesome in that movie that came out a while back." He snapped his fingers again. "Let me see if I can remember the name of it...something about the pharaohs, right? I should remember 'cause I've seen it four or five times. You looked so good in that Egyptian outfit. I wish I could—"

"The chief," Suzanne interrupted. "You were going to get the chief for us, remember?"

He grinned. "Of course. I'll be right back."

"Ignoramus," Suzanne muttered after he left. "Where do they recruit the cops around here? The zoo?"

A few moments later Chief Bowers ambled up to the car. "You shouldn't be here," he said gruffly. "Go home."

"Excuse me, but I think that's pretty damn rude," Suzanne told him. "Can't you tell how distraught A.J. is? She just wants to know if this has anything to do with Sara. All you have to do is tell her it doesn't and we'll be on our way."

Chief Bower's weathered face showed no sign of emotion, but the way he hesitated before speaking confirmed my fear.

"It's Sara, isn't it?" I heard myself say, although I really didn't want to know the answer.

He avoided eye contact with me. "I suggest you go back to your house and stay there," he said. "I'll come by just as soon as I can."

Suzanne's face lost its color. She must have realized the same thing I did—he didn't want to come out and tell us Sara was dead.

I curled my fingers into a tight knot in my lap, trying to keep them from shaking. "I want to see her," I said. "I want to see my baby."

"Ms. Jenkins, please," Chief Bowers said. "Take my advice and go home. Let us do our job."

"No, I want to be with her!" I said it so loud that it made Suzanne jump. A wave of hysteria washed over me, forcing me to do something—anything—but sit in the car.

I undid my seatbelt, got out, and walked briskly toward the marina.

"Ms. Jenkins, I beg you to stop!" Chief Bowers called after me.

I quickened my pace, driven by a force too primal to ignore.

The docks were just a few yards away when I felt two arms reach around my waist and lift me off the ground.

"You don't want to go down there," Chief Bowers said as I struggled to break free from him. "Now listen to me and go home or I'm going to cuff you."

I kicked my feet and strained against his powerful arms. It was no use—he had me in a vise grip.

"I'll settle down if you'll be honest with me," I said, panting. "Was the girl you found Sara?"

"You promise to stay still and not run away from me if I tell you?" he asked.

I nodded and relaxed my limbs. "I promise. Now please tell me."

He set me down gently and unwrapped his arms from around my waist. As I turned to face him, Suzanne caught up with us.

"You better keep your hands off of her!" she said, wagging her finger at him. "Or I'll tell the media you were using excessive force!"

Chief Bowers ignored her and said to me, "Here's what we know so far—a fisherman found a body in the river this morning. It was lying on an oyster bed exposed by the low tide."

"A girl?" Suzanne asked.

He sighed and nodded. "A teen. We haven't been able to positively identify her yet, so don't jump to conclusions."

"What was she wearing?" I asked.

He frowned. "Ms. Jenkins, please—"

"What was she wearing, godammit!" I demanded.

The look on his face told me the answer.

Too many emotions hit me at once. I became lightheaded, dizzy. Despite the heat of the morning, I shivered and felt my skin go cold.

"A.J., you don't look so good," Suzanne said.

My knees became liquid, no longer able to support me.

The last thing I heard before everything turned black was Suzanne shouting, "Don't let her fall!"

chapter 20

I CAME TO, and found myself gazing up at the face of a handsome man.

His raven hair was pulled back into a ponytail, his skin was bronzed, and a few days of stubble peppered his angular chin. He smiled, caressed my cheek with the back of his hand, and asked me, "You okay, baby?"

I tried to raise my head. It wouldn't budge.

The handsome man—aka Randy Reynolds, my ex-husband—leaned down and kissed my cheek. "Don't try to move, baby," he said to me. "You're strapped to a gurney and your neck is in a cervical brace."

I wanted to tell him to stop calling me baby, but I couldn't find my voice.

"Do you know where you are?" he asked.

Behind him was a blue sky dotted with puffy clouds. I assumed it meant I was still outside, at the marina.

I swallowed a couple of times and managed to eke out a question: "What are you doing here?"

"Looking after you, I suppose," he said with a grin. "My plane landed in Charleston about an hour ago. I was on my way to the beach house when Suzanne called and told me to come here to the marina instead. Seems you fainted and hit the back of your head on the pavement pretty hard. You've been in and out of consciousness ever since."

Another face appeared next to Randy's. It was a young man with curly blonde hair to die for. He identified himself as Jeff Chopin, a paramedic.

"How are you feeling, Ms. Jenkins?" he asked.

The back of my head throbbed and I felt queasy. But I told him I was fine, hoping he would believe me and unstrap me from the gurney.

No such luck. He called out for his partner, then he said to me, "We're going to take you to the ambulance now and transport you to the hospital so you can get a thorough exam."

"No," I protested, my voice growing stronger but sounding as raspy as Suzanne's. "I don't want to go to the hospital. I have to stay here and talk to Chief Bowers."

Suzanne's face appeared in my narrow field of vision, lower and closer than the others. "Hey, girl," she said. "You gave me quite a scare. I thought you busted your head open."

"Where's Chief Bowers?" I asked her.

She gave me an eye roll. "You mean Andy Griffith? He's being tight-lipped and won't tell me a damn thing. And he said he'd arrest my ass if I got anywhere near the docks. So you might as well go on to the hospital and get checked out. You're not missing anything here."

"No, I need to stay. I've got to find out what's going on."

Jeff, my blonde Adonis of a paramedic, shook his head. "Ms. Jenkins you may have suffered a concussion. It's imperative that you go to the hospital right away and get a CAT scan."

"Yeah, you might have brain damage," Randy said with a wink. "Even more than usual."

I shot him a dirty look and resolved to my fate.

The next few hours were pure torture. All I could think about while the doctors examined, probed, and prodded my body was Sara and what I would do if something terrible had happened to her.

I also prayed, more than I had ever prayed in my life. For the most part they were silent prayers, but at one point Randy joined me as I asked the Lord to please, please not let the girl they found in the river be Sara. It was the first time I'd seen Randy shed a tear since his father's death.

It was around noon when the doctors released me, apparently satisfied that I hadn't suffered any permanent damage to my brain. They told me to go home, go to bed, get plenty of rest, and to keep an ice pack on the back of my head so the hematoma I'd gotten wouldn't grow to the size of a melon.

But when we got back to the house I was in no mood to lie around and do nothing. I wanted to call Chief Bowers NOW and find out what the hell was going on. Randy and Suzanne wouldn't let me, though. They both insisted that I wait for the chief to come to the house as promised and insisted that I get in bed and rest.

"C'mon, girl, you're going to put that ice pack on your head and chill," Randy said as he led me by the arm to my bedroom. I couldn't get over how calm he seemed, how in control of his emotions he was. Here I was falling apart at the seams, but he was as rock steady as ever. He had to be hurting inside like me; he had to be worried to death over Sara's fate, but there was no visible sign of it—except the one time he broke down crying when we prayed together at the hospital. I figured he must be doing it for me; he was trying to stay strong for both of us so I would have a shoulder to lean on. I might have admired him for it if it weren't for the fact that he had screwed up my life—and Sara's.

"I'm going to give you those pills the doctor gave you," he said, tucking me into bed. "They'll kill the pain and help you relax."

He left for a moment and came back with the pills and the ice pack.

I don't know if he gave me more of the pain killers than he should have, but they knocked me out cold.

It was four in the afternoon when he shook me awake.

"Chief Bowers is here," he said. "Do you feel up to talking to him?"

What a dumb question. I threw the covers off and scurried into the living room.

Chief Bowers was sitting across the dining table from Suzanne. I tried to read his face, but it was as stoic as ever.

He gave me a nod. "Afternoon, Ms. Jenkins. I bet you have one heck of a headache, don't you? That was quite a fall you took."

"Forget that," I said, thinking he was a moron for trying to make small talk when so much was at stake. "Just tell me what you know about Sara."

"Well, I can tell you this—the girl we found this morning isn't her."

I almost collapsed to my knees with relief. "Thank you, God," I whispered, and let out a long breath.

Chief Bowers gestured to the chair next to him. "Please have a seat. There's a lot we need to discuss."

He pulled the chair out for me, and as I settled into it Randy took the seat next to Suzanne.

"So do you have any leads on Sara's whereabouts?" Randy asked the chief.

He didn't answer him. Instead, he reached for the briefcase at his feet.

"Folks, I have something to share with you that you're going to find quite disturbing," he said as he placed the briefcase on the table. He unlatched it and took out a manila envelope.

Randy and I exchanged worried glances.

Chief Bowers continued, "Ms. Jenkins, you said Sara was wearing a T-shirt on the night she disappeared...is that correct?"

I nodded. "A pink one with 'Surfing Diva' embroidered on it. It's one of her favorites."

He opened the envelope and took out an 8X10 photo. He sat it in front of me and asked, "Is this the T-shirt?"

I sucked in my breath. It was a close-up of Sara's shirt, laid out on a gray metallic table. Blood stains were visible near the collar.

"Dear God, what is this?" I gasped.

"Ms. Jenkins, I know how hard this is," Chief Bowers began. "But can you positively identify the shirt? Is it the one Sara was wearing?"

My eyes flooded with tears and my throat burned with fear.

"I'll take your reaction as a yes," Chief Bowers said dryly.

Randy looked at me. For the first time I could see worry in his eyes. "What the hell is going on?" he asked Chief Bowers. "Why do you have my daughter's shirt?"

Chief Bowers didn't answer right away. He took his time putting the photo back into the envelope and putting the envelope back into the briefcase. Finally, he cleared his throat and said, "We found the shirt this morning. It's being processed for fingerprints and DNA evidence."

"Where the hell did you find it?" Randy asked. He now looked visibly shaken.

The answer Chief Bowers gave him caused a stunned silence to hang over the table: "We found it on the girl we recovered from the river this morning. She was wearing it."

chapter 21

It was Suzanne who asked Chief Bowers the question that was on all of our minds: "Why in the world would that girl be wearing Sara's shirt?"

Chief Bowers folded his hands on the table. "That's the million dollar question, isn't it? I have a theory, but first let me fill you in on some details about the girl. She's a seventeen year-old runaway—been missing from her home in Alabama for three weeks now. They think her boyfriend brought her here since he has relatives who live at the beach. But the relatives deny ever seeing him or the girl. Anyway, the terrible thing is the girl was murdered in cold blood. Shot in the back of the head, execution style."

Suzanne's hand flew to her mouth. "Oh my God, that's horrible. So do you think she got dumped in the river? Is that how she wound up there?"

I tried hard to concentrate on what they were saying, but my mind was spinning out of control. What did all this mean? Was Sara in the hands of a murderer? And if she wasn't wearing her shirt that meant the bastard who had her had stripped her. And if he'd stripped her that meant he might have...

I choked back the bile rising in my throat.

"Here's what we think," Chief Bowers continued. "Her body was deliberately placed on the oyster bank. The murderer wanted us to find her."

"And find Sara's shirt," Randy said, balling his hands into a fist. "If I ever get hold of the sick son of a bitch who did this, I'll kill him!"

"Off the record, I wouldn't stop you," Chief Bowers said. "I just hope I get the pleasure of doing it first."

Suzanne said, "I'm sorry, but I don't get any of this. Why would this sicko *want* you to find Sara's shirt?"

"It's a message," Chief Bowers said. "He wants us to know he has her."

Randy slammed a fist down on the table, startling all of us. "So what does he want? A ransom? Hell, I'll be glad to give the bastard every dollar I have to get Sara back."

"Let's hope he does want a ransom," Chief Bowers said. "That way he'll make contact with us and give us a chance to track him."

A ransom, I thought. If only it were that simple. There wasn't a thing I owned that I wouldn't give in exchange for Sara, including my life. But I had the feeling her captor was after something other than money. Just like I had a feeling that Alex Saunders was hiding something.

Thinking about that caused me to ask Chief Bowers if the CSI people had confirmed the blood on the blanket was Sara's.

"Not yet," he replied. "They're still processing the hairs we got from Sara's hair brush to determine if it's a DNA match, but it will take a few more days to get the results back." He lowered his voice and asked me, "Where is Alex, anyway?"

I was about to answer, but Suzanne beat me to it. "He's in his room," she said. "The poor kid is scared to death—wouldn't even come out to eat today. I think he's afraid he's going to be arrested."

As he should be, I thought.

"Is his father coming to get him?" Chief Bowers asked her.

"Yeah. I'm surprised he hasn't got here yet."

Chief Bowers kept his voice low as he said, "We may need to keep Alex around a bit longer. Something else has come up that makes things more complicated."

"I knew it," I said. "That kid's been hiding something. I can see it in his eyes."

"That may be true," Chief Bowers said. "We discovered semen stains on the blanket. The assumption, of course, is that it came from him."

I looked at him incredulously. "Semen? You mean you think he had sex with Sara?"

Randy gave me a dirty look that implied it was my fault this had happened.

"We can't answer that simply based on the evidence," Chief Bowers explained. "Just like we can't answer if they had consensual sex or…"

"Or if Sara was raped," I finished for him, feeling my blood pressure rise to astronomical proportions.

"Those are conclusions we can't jump to," he said. "That's why I need to talk to Alex and see what he has to say about it."

"Why don't you just take the little bastard in?" I said. "This proves he's been lying. Can't you charge him with something?"

"Not at this time," he said, standing. "Plus he's a minor—that makes things even trickier. We have to proceed cautiously."

Suzanne shook her head. "This doesn't make sense. Despite what A.J. thinks, Alex would never hurt Sara. Besides, he sure as hell didn't shoot that girl in the back of the head and dress her in Sara's shirt. So you're barking up the wrong tree by thinking he's guilty."

"I'm not saying he's guilty of killing the girl," Chief Bowers told her. "But I agree with Ms. Jenkins that there's *something* he's not telling us. And we can't rule out the possibility that all this began with something that happened between him and Sara on the beach. So if you'll excuse me, I'm going to go have a little chat with the boy." He looked at me and said, "Would you mind showing me to his room?"

He followed me to the guest room. The door was unlocked, so I pushed it open.

We both stood there with our jaws agape.

No Alex. Just an empty room with the window open, screen removed.

"I'll be damned. He ran away," Chief Bowers grunted.

I crossed my arms. "And that could only mean one thing... he really *does* have something to hide."

chapter 22

"So what do you make of all this?" Randy asked me after Chief Bowers left.

He followed me into the living room and we sat on the sofa. "You know as much as I do," I said, wincing from a throbbing headache.

"Do you think Sara had sex with Alex?"

I let out a long sigh as I mulled it over. "I don't think so. She's never come right out and said it, but I think she wants to hold on to her virginity. So if there was any sex going on, I'm sure Alex must have forced it on her."

"Or they could have been making out and Alex got a bit too excited," Randy said. "It happens to guys sometimes, you know. Especially when they're that young."

I closed my eyes, trying not to think about it. "No matter what, *something* must have happened to make Alex run. I've had a hunch all along that he's been hiding something."

Randy was quiet for a moment, like he was lost in thought. In the silence I heard Suzanne rummaging around in the kitchen. The refrigerator door opened and closed. Then I heard her call out, "Is there anything around here to eat besides frozen pizza?

And we're getting really low on beer. Someone's going to have to make a run to the store. You want me to do it?"

"No," Randy told her sharply. "Nobody's going anywhere. The media and the paparazzi are everywhere on the island, especially outside the front door. So we're going to batten down the hatches and stay in here with the curtains drawn and the doors locked. And I've already arranged for a security detail to guard the house. There should be a man watching the front and another one watching the rear and the beach."

I looked at him with narrowed eyes and said, "So I guess that means I'm a prisoner in my own house, huh?"

"For now," he said. "It's for your own good. There's no telling what kind of nut cases are going to come out of the woodwork now that Sara's disappearance has made the headlines."

"Well, I can't live on frozen pizza," Suzanne said, walking into the living room. "And I'm so stressed that I'm going to need more than just a few beers. So *somebody* has to get some food and stuff for us."

"I'll see to it," Randy said, inching closer to me to give Suzanne room on the sofa. "I'll have one of the guys from the security force make a run for us."

"Make sure he gets beer," Suzanne said, hands on hips. "Or something even stronger. If not, I'm going to implode."

Randy chuckled and patted the empty cushion next to him. "You want to take a load off?"

She shook her head. "Naw, I'm getting cramps. It's that time of the month. I think I'll lie down for a while."

She went upstairs, and I waited for Randy to scoot his butt away from me.

But he didn't.

"Um, you want to give me some room?" I asked.

He grinned. "Sorry...old habits are hard to break, I guess." He slid across the sofa to the opposite end. "There, is that better?"

I nodded.

"Give me your feet," he said.

I cocked an eyebrow. "Excuse me?"

"I know how stressed out you are, so let me massage your feet to help you relax."

It was tempting, but I said, "Randy, we're divorced. Divorced people don't rub each other's feet."

"Says who? It's the least I can do for you." Without warning, he grabbed my legs and raised them to the sofa. Then he placed my bare feet in his lap and began squeezing my toes.

It felt so good. But it also felt so wrong.

"This isn't right," I protested. "Not with Sara in danger." I jerked my feet from him and placed them on the floor.

He looked surprised. "I just thought it might help to get your mind off things for a while."

"I don't want my mind off them—not until Sara is safe."

He slumped low and blew out some air. "You know, there's one thing I don't get about all this." He cut his dark eyes at me. "I know how good of a mother you are. So why didn't you know Sara didn't come home that night?"

I looked away from him. "I was tired, Randy. I fell asleep."

"Yeah, but I know you—you worry yourself to death whenever she's out with Alex. I can't imagine you sleeping through the night without waking up at least once to check on her."

My throat tightened and I clasped my hands together to keep them from shaking. I had never been a good liar and this was no exception.

"I fell asleep and that's all there is to it," I snapped. "So let it drop."

"Okay, okay, don't get so pissed off. I'm just trying to get my head wrapped around this thing, that's all."

I heard my cell phone ring. I jumped up from the sofa and hurried into the bedroom to answer it.

The caller ID displayed 'Unknown.' A twinge of apprehension twisted in the pit of my stomach as I brought the phone to my lips and said hello.

"A.J., it's me," Drew answered. "I wanted to call and see how you're doing. I heard about Sara on the news. I can't tell you how sorry I am."

I sat on the edge of the bed and cupped a hand around my mouth, hoping Randy wouldn't hear me say, "Thanks for calling. I'm trying to keep things quiet about us. There's no use in you getting dragged into this, Drew. The media's going to be all over it. So keep your distance, okay?"

"But I feel like I need to be there with you. I want to comfort you."

"That's sweet of you, but I have plenty of people here to help me through this. So it's best if you don't—"

Randy walked into the bedroom. "Who's on the phone?" he asked.

"Just a friend," I said. "They want to see how I'm doing."

"What friend? Anyone I know?"

"No. I met them recently."

He gave me a suspicious nod and went back into the living room.

I put my mouth close to the phone. "Drew, just do as I say and lay low. You don't want to end up in some gossip magazine do you? It wouldn't be good for your medical practice."

"Actually it might," he said with a chuckle. "It might give me some publicity. But seriously, I feel like I should be with you."

"Maybe when this is over," I said.

"And it will be. Soon. I'm sure you're going to find Sara and she'll be safe and sound."

I wanted to believe him, but knowing she was in the hands of a sociopath who had already proved he could kill in cold blood brought another round of tears to my eyes.

"I have to go now," I told Drew. Thanks for calling."

"I'm here for you, A.J.," he said. "We were meant to be together. Don't ever forget that."

He disconnected, leaving me with a strange, uneasy feeling.

chapter 23

I WOKE THE next morning to the sound of something crashing.

It sounded like it came from the kitchen, so I put on my robe and headed that way.

I found Randy bent over at the waist, picking up the shattered pieces of a coffee cup.

"Sorry," he said when he saw me. "It slipped from my hand. Good thing I hadn't poured any coffee into it yet."

I glanced at the digital clock above the range—7:15 A.M—and did a quick mental calculation of how many hours Sara had been missing.

Was it really only forty-eight? It felt more like an eternity had passed since I'd last seen her. And how much longer was this hell going to last before...

"You doing okay?" Randy asked, drawing me away from my thoughts.

"Define okay," I replied with a sigh.

He emptied the remains of the coffee cup into the waste basket under the sink. His hair was loose, no longer in a pony tail, and hung around his shoulders like black wool. When he turned from the waste basket and faced me, I noticed his eyes had dark circles under them. Like me, he probably hadn't slept well.

"I'm telling you, A.J., this thing is killing me," he said. "I've never felt so powerless in my life. I wish we could do something besides sit around and wait."

I reached into a cabinet and took out two mugs. "Maybe we should do a press conference," I suggested. "We can make a plea to Sara's captor to let her go." I handed him one of the mugs and poured some coffee into mine.

"Like that would make a difference," Randy snorted. "I don't think that sicko has any human feelings we can appeal to. But if you want to try, I'm gain." He poured his coffee and took a peek through the mini-blinds out the window. "We won't have far to go to do the press conference. It looks like every major network and local TV station has a van parked across the street."

I took a look and saw that he was right. CNN, NBC, ABC, CBS, Fox News—they were all there, waiting for something to happen. Knowing them, they were probably hoping it would be something tragic; something that would attract more viewers and give them higher ratings.

I closed the min-blinds in disgust.

"This is just a soap opera to them, isn't it?" I said to Randy.

He took a sip of coffee. "They're just doing their job. If people weren't curious, they wouldn't be here."

Suzanne walked quietly into the kitchen, wearing her pink robe and a frown on her face. She, too, had dark circles under her eyes.

"I didn't sleep a wink," she said as she made her way to the refrigerator. She opened it and looked inside. "Nothing but frozen pizza and some lunch meat. This sucks. When are we going to get some food and booze?"

"I've got a guy bringing us some groceries today," Randy told her. "But no booze. We need to keep our heads straight."

She slammed the refrigerator door shut. "Then give me some of those pills the doctor gave A.J. yesterday. I can't deal with all this shit going on without something to cushion it."

I heard my cell phone ring in the bedroom. Randy and I exchanged nervous glances.

"Go get it quick," he said. "You never know when Sara's captor might try to make contact with us."

I ran to the bedroom and looked at the caller ID. It read Paul Saunders—Alex's father.

"Paul, have you talked to Alex?" I said anxiously into the phone, skipping formalities.

"Hello, sweetheart," he said in a deep and steady voice. "First, let me tell you how sorry I am to hear about Sara. And to answer your question, yes I've talked to Alex. He called me this morning."

"What did he tell you? Why did he run?" I couldn't get the words out quick enough.

"He's scared, A.J. He thinks they're going to put him in jail. He said he's still in Charleston, but he won't tell me where."

"Do you know they found blood on the blanket he was sharing with Sara? And now they say they found semen on it too."

Randy approached me and whispered, "Who is it?" I silently mouthed Paul's name. He nodded and stood close to me so he could listen in.

"I know about the blood," Paul said on the other end of the phone. "But Alex swears he doesn't have a clue why it's there. And as far as the semen goes...no, I didn't know about that. But I have a pretty good idea what might have happened."

"I'm all ears," I told him.

He cleared his voice and said, "Alex let me know that he and Sara stayed after the fireworks show to talk and look at the stars. Then they moved to a more secluded spot behind the dunes to...well, you know...make out."

I winced. "Funny, he didn't mention anything to me about that part."

"I don't think I would have, either," Paul said with a laugh. "It's not exactly the kind of thing you brag about to your girl-friend's mother. Anyway, he said things got kinda hot and heavy between him and Sara and he begged her to let him go all the way. She told him no and they ended up arguing over it. He said Sara got so mad that she told him she was going home. He was so pissed that he told her to go. So she left. That's the last he saw of her."

My blood boiled. "You mean your asshole of a son let my daughter walk home in the dark, knowing other girls had gone missing out here?" I wanted to scream, to throw the phone clear across the room. "How could he be so stupid?"

"Baby, try to settle down," Randy whispered.

I shot him a dirty look.

"I'm so sorry he did that," Paul said. "And I agree with you—he's an asshole for letting her walk home in the dark. But you have to remember he would never intentionally hurt Sara."

"How do you explain the semen, then?" I asked, still furi-ous. "You said Sara refused to have sex with him, so how did *that* get there?"

He hesitated before answering. "I think it's one of two things. Either they fooled around to the point of him ejaculating, or he did what boys his age are prone to do when they're alone and feel sexually frustrated...if you get my drift."

The image that popped into my head of Alex whacking off made me want to puke.

"But you don't know this for sure," I said. "Alex is nothing but a liar. How do we know he's not making this all up?"

"I know my son," Paul said flatly. "I trust him on this one."

"Have you contacted the police? Have you told them you've talked to him?" I asked.

"No. But I suppose you will, won't you?"

"Yes, Paul, I'll tell them if you don't. They need to know everything." I realized how hypocritical I was being. If anyone was guilty of withholding information, it was me. Maybe I should listen to my own advice.

"Again, I'm sorry for all this," Paul said. "You know how much you and Sara mean to me. If there's anything I can do, please let me know." He paused and added, "Oh, by the way, your concert sales numbers are in and they're through the roof. And your new album just went multi-platinum. Congratulations, sweetheart."

"I don't give a damn about any of that," I said quietly. "It means nothing to me without Sara."

"I understand. Just thought you'd like to know."

My ears picked up a sound in the distance. I kept silent and listened.

"A.J.? You still there?" Paul asked.

Randy gave me a curious look. "You okay?" he asked.

The sound grew louder.

I dropped the phone to the floor.

Sirens. Lots of sirens. And they were approaching fast.

chapter 24

"YOU'RE NOT CHASING after those cops again," Randy said as he followed me to the kitchen. "So don't even think about it."

I ignored him and peeked through the blinds. Just like the day before, I watched one cruiser after another fly past the house.

"Do you think they found another body?" I asked him.

He was about to answer when Suzanne called out for us from the living room. "Guys, come here quick!" she shouted. "They're interrupting the *Early Show* to do a live local report from Folly Beach. They say they've got some breaking news on Sara's disappearance!"

Randy and I rushed into the living room just as a female reporter appeared on the screen. It looked like she was standing at the entrance to the county park. Suzanne turned up the volume with the remote, and I held my breath as I listened to the reporter say, "Details are sketchy at this time, but we'll tell you what we have been able to learn so far. A call was received by the Folly Beach Police Department about a body being discovered here at the west end of the beach, near the county park. An eyewitness said the body was found in a shallow grave near the dunes. It's unknown if the body is a male or female, or if it is related to the story we have been closely following since yesterday—the disappearance of Sara Michelle Reynolds, the teenage daughter of one of America's most beloved singer-songwriters, A.J., and her divorced rock star husband, Randy Reynolds. As you may recall, Sara is the third teenager to go missing here at Folly in the past few weeks. And, sadly, one girl—a runaway teen from Alabama—was found shot to death in the Folly River yesterday. Of course, the question on everyone's mind is if these cases are related—something police won't confirm or deny. But the discovery of this second body has many wondering if there is a serial killer on the loose on this once peaceful island. We'll keep you updated as more details become available. For Live Five News, this is Emma Rogers, reporting from Folly Beach."

chapter 25

It was just after noon when the doorbell rang.

Randy let Chief Bowers in. He carried a briefcase, his face long and sullen. As usual, he suggested we sit at the dining table. As usual, I dreaded what he was about to say.

"Let me offer you some relief," he began as soon as we were settled. "The girl they found buried in the sand this morning isn't Sara. It's a young lady named Shelly Perkins."

I recognized the name. "That's one of the girls I saw on the poster at Bert's. One of the missing girls, right?" I asked.

"That's correct, Ms. Jenkins. A man walking his dog came across the body this morning. And when I say she was buried in the sand it's a bit of a stretch—she was only *covered* with sand. In fact, her feet were still showing."

"Crap," Randy said. "It sounds like someone wanted her to be found—just like the girl yesterday."

"Indeed," Chief Bowers said. "And she was murdered the same way—gunshot to the back of the head."

"So the deaths must be related," Suzanne said. "Does that mean we really do have a serial killer on our hands?"

"Unfortunately, it's beginning to look that way," Chief Bowers said with a frown.

I wanted to ask him if the girl was wearing any of Sara's clothes. But I couldn't bring myself to utter the words.

"I need to change subjects for a moment," Chief Bowers said. He took his briefcase from the floor and placed it on the table. As he unlatched it, he looked at me and said, "Ms. Jenkins, have you been completely honest with me about your whereabouts on the night Sara went missing?"

My pulse raced. "What do you mean?" I asked as innocently as possible.

"It's a simple question," he said, taking out a manila envelope from the briefcase. He sat it in front of me without opening it. "Were you here like you claimed to be, or were you somewhere else?"

It felt like I was on trial. I wondered if I should take advantage of my Miranda rights and remain silent.

"I think you'll find something in the envelope that will jog your memory," Chief Bowers said, the hint of a smirk on his face.

"What the hell is he talking about?" Randy asked me.

I looked across the table into his searching eyes. "I'm sorry," was all I could say.

"Sorry for what?" He turned his gaze to Chief Bowers. "Would you please tell me what's going on?"

"Open the envelope, Ms. Jenkins," he said. "Then try telling me the truth for a change."

Inside the envelope was the morning edition of the *Post and Courier*. On the front page was a headline that asked: *Was A.J. With a Stranger on the Night of Her Daughter's Disappearance?* Below it was a photo of Drew and me kissing on the pier, fireworks exploding in the background.

"What the hell?" Randy gasped.

"Goddamn paparazzi," Suzanne muttered.

I couldn't speak; all I could do was stare at the photo.

Chief Bowers said, "Since it's impossible to be in two places at once, I have to assume you've been lying about being home that night. Is that right, Ms. Jenkins?"

"A.J., who the hell is this guy?" Randy demanded. "And why are you kissing him?"

"He's a friend," I said, choking on my words. "A friend I was trying to protect."

"Please elaborate," Chief Bowers urged me.

My eyes were still glued to the photo as I said, "He's a doctor—he lives here at the beach. I met him on the interstate...he was kind enough to change a flat tire for me. Then we ran into each other a few times after that."

"Looks like you were doing more than running into each other," Randy snarled.

"And how were you trying to protect him?" Chief Bowers asked.

"I didn't want something like this to happen," I explained. "I didn't want him to show up in the gossip magazines. I knew the media would have a heyday over our relationship, especially with Sara missing. But he has nothing to do with it." I raised my eyes and looked at Chief Bowers. "I promise you, he has nothing to do with Sara's disappearance."

"And how can you be so sure?"

I lowered my gaze. "Because I spent most of that night with him."

"Great, just great," Randy hissed. "So you were screwing this guy's brains out instead of watching Sara." He shook his head in disgust. "And I thought you were a good mother."

I ignored him and told Chief Bowers, "I'm sorry I lied. But it was for a good reason. I hope you can understand that."

"And I hope you understand how important it is to be honest with me," he said, gathering the newspaper and putting it back into the briefcase. "You do want to find your daughter, don't you?"

I looked at him incredulously. "Of course, I do. How can you ask me a question like that?"

"Because we can't leave any stone unturned in this investigation. So I'm going to need the doctor's name and address."

"Why? I already told you he has nothing to do with Sara's disappearance. Why can't you leave him alone?"

He took a notepad from the briefcase and opened it to a blank page. "Let me ask you something," he said as he scribbled something down. "You said you were with him most of the night. Exactly how long was that?"

"It was around three in the morning when I got back home," I answered honestly.

"And what were you doing before then?"

I didn't want to look at Randy, yet I found my eyes drawn to him. His face was flush, his jaw set. He shook his head and looked away.

"We talked and had a couple of drinks," I said. "Then we..."

"Made love?" Chief Bowers guessed.

I nodded.

"Did you fall asleep while you were with him?" he asked.

What a curious question, I thought. "I may have dozed off for a while. But what's that got to do with anything?"

He didn't look up from his pad. "That means there was a period of time when you didn't know the doctor's whereabouts."

I almost laughed outloud. "Are you kidding me? He was right there, next to me. He didn't go anywhere."

"How do you know that if you were asleep?"

"Oh, this is ridiculous," I said. "The man is a doctor. You act like he's some kind of suspect."

He looked up from the pad. "I need his name and address. I think it's time for me to pay your doctor a little visit."

chapter 26

THAT AFTERNOON MRS. Turner brought us a casserole for supper. Tuna noodle. Not my favorite, but I was thankful for her thoughtfulness.

She didn't stay long, and after she left I busied myself by cleaning the house. I found that doing simple, everyday things like sweeping and dusting took my mind off of Sara, at least momentarily. But then thoughts of her being tortured, raped, or even worse flooded my consciousness, unleashing yet another round of tears.

And I felt trapped, like a chick in an egg. The walls of the house were closing in on me and there was nothing I could do about it. The screen porch was off limits. The window blinds were drawn. No fresh air, no salty breeze. Outside was a beach packed with people soaking up the sun and frolicking in the warm surf. But inside it felt like the dead of winter.

A tomb.

Yes, that's what it was, a tomb. A place where my soul was slowly dying, coming closer to annihilation with each visit from Chief Bowers. Two girls murdered, two left. It was now down to a fifty-fifty chance that Sara would be next. And if she were, it would be the end of me. No more songs, no more concerts, no more albums. I might survive physically, but it would do me in psychologically. Of that I was certain. No way could I deal with another tragedy of that magnitude in my life. I would shrink into a shell and stay there for the rest of my days.

Without Sara, there would be nothing but darkness.

I was sitting on my bed, thinking about all this, when Randy entered without knocking.

It was the first time I'd seen him since Chief Bower's visit. He had gone straight to the downstairs guest room afterwards and had remained there until now.

My body stiffened as he sat next to me.

"We have a lot to discuss," he began, gazing straight ahead. "I wanted to wait until I calmed down to talk to you."

I let out a long sigh. "I'm sorry I lied to you. But I did it for a good reason."

He snickered. "Yeah, so you could protect your new lover. Way to go, A.J. You picked a hell of a time to get horny."

"If you came in here to get in my face about that, you can leave," I snapped.

He shook his head. "I just can't get over you doing something like that. It's so out of character for you."

"I'm divorced, remember? I can sleep with anyone I want to, anytime I want to. At least I waited until I was single again. Unlike *someone* I know."

"That may very well be, but at least none of my flings ended up with our daughter going missing."

I rose to my feet. "So now you're blaming the whole thing on me? Is that right?"

He shrugged. "It happened on your watch, that's all I know. And the way it's beginning to look to me, you weren't watching at all."

My eyes flared with rage. "What the hell is that supposed to mean?"

He stood to face me. "It means you were flat on your back with your legs spread wide open when you should have been paying more attention to what was going on with Sara."

"You son of a bitch!" I slapped him hard across the cheek.

He didn't flinch. Instead, he grabbed my wrists and demanded, "Who the hell is this guy? Where did you meet him?"

I struggled to break free, but his grip was too strong. "He's a doctor. And he's a much better lover than you ever were!"

It was a lie; Randy was actually a better lover than Drew. But I was so pissed off that I wanted to hurt his pride.

He squeezed my wrists until I cried out in pain. With his forehead pressed against mine he said, "Oh, really? Maybe if you'd been around more often you would have known how good of a lover I can be. But you were more interested in your music, weren't you?"

"You were gone just as much as I was," I fired back, "and if anyone's to blame for Sara's disappearance, it's you!"

"How the hell do you figure that?"

"Because you're the one who had to screw up our lives by cheating on me! If it hadn't been for that we would have never been here this week! I would have never had to reach out to her and try to get her to love me again!"

He loosened his grip on my wrists. "Love you again? She never stopped loving you, A.J. Why would you say something like that?"

"Because she blames me for the divorce," I said, crying in spite of myself. "She hasn't been the same since. That's why I wanted to bring her here and spend some time alone with her."

He let go of me. "This is stupid. We're beating each other up when we should be working together. This fussing and fighting is going to do nothing to bring her home. We need to think of something we can do to help."

"I already told you what we need to do—have a press conference. Let's do it today. Let's offer a million dollars...two million dollars. I don't care as long as it brings her back."

He raked his fingers through his hair. "I'll do it if you want me to. But I don't think it's going to make a difference."

I let out a frustrated sigh. "Why? You just said we need to do something. That would be doing *something*, wouldn't it? We can't just sit around here and wait. It's driving me crazy!"

His eyes turned tender. "I know it is. It's driving all of us crazy. And how do you think I feel, knowing I'm her father and there's not a damn thing I can do to protect her. I hate to tell you this, but I punched a hole in the wall of the guest room a little while ago. I was thinking about her being with that monster and what he might be doing to her."

His eyes reddened. My first impulse was to lace my arms around his neck, to whisper that I understood. But the pain he'd caused me over the years trumped my desire to comfort him.

"I don't understand why you're reluctant to do the press conference," I said. "Maybe that's what her captor wants. Maybe that's why he dressed that girl in Sara's shirt. He might want us to offer him a ransom. It's worth a try, isn't it?"

He raised the corners of his lips into a sad, reluctant smile. "Sure, it's worth a try. But you have to understand that we're dealing with a sociopathic killer, A.J. He may not respond to offers of money. He might be playing a sick game and Sara's just a pawn in it. We have to prepare ourselves for the worst."

"No! Stop saying that!" I turned away from him. "We have to try, Randy. We have to try."

He came up behind me and put a hand on my shoulder. "I'm just being realistic. I don't want you—"

"Dammit, do you want to start planning her funeral?" I spun around to face him. "Is that what you want? Well, I'm not ready to give up yet! So I'll do the press conference without you if I have to!"

"A.J., please—"

"Excuse me," Suzanne's voice rang out. She stood in the doorway with her cell phone in her hand. "I hate to interrupt a good argument, but there's someone on the phone I think you ought to talk to, A.J."

I strode over to her. "Who is it?"

She bit her lower lip. "I know you're going to think I'm crazy, but I called my psychic back in Hollywood. Her name is Mrs. Gaylord. I told her about Sara and she immediately got a vision. Now she wants to talk to you."

I almost told her not to waste my time. But I was so desperate that I took the phone and said hello.

"A.J., I'm Amanda Gaylord," a commanding voice informed me. "Suzanne filled me in on what happened. I'm so sorry that you are going through this. It must be exhausting physically and emotionally."

"You have no idea," I said.

"I want to help. I'll even waive my fee. I never charge for missing children…it seems immoral."

"Thank you," I said, wondering who this woman was. There were plenty of so-called celebrity psychics in Hollywood, but I had never heard of this one.

"The Spirits have already sent me a vision pertaining to Sara," she went on to say. "First, I want to let you know that she is alive and in good health. But she is in grave danger. The person who has her is a tormented soul, capable of anything."

"Do you have any idea where she is?" I asked.

"I'm afraid not. I see a dark place, but I'm afraid that's all. I need to come there—to feel her clothing, to get closer to her vibration. I can catch a flight right away. Of course, I must ask you to pay the fare. I'm willing to fly coach if you like."

I scratched my head. "Um, I don't know. I mean, I'm sure you're a good psychic and all, but—"

"I promise I will help you find Sara," she cut in. "I'll do a lot more than the police have."

That wouldn't take much, I thought, looking at Suzanne. She whispered, "Do it. She's really good. She predicted I would go to jail before it happened."

Anyone could have seen that coming, I thought.

"Okay, Mrs. Gaylord, I'll fly you here," I said. "Don't worry about contacting the airlines; I'll charter a flight for you. Suzanne will give you all the details."

I handed Suzanne the phone.

A psychic.

It was a long shot, but at this point I was willing to grasp at straws, since I had a feeling time was running out for Sara.

chapter 27

RANDY MADE ARRANGEMENTS for our press conference to go live at five o'clock that afternoon. In a way, I looked forward to it, hoping against hope that I could find a way to convince Sara's captor to let her go. In another way I dreaded it, knowing I would be bombarded with questions about Drew and out relationship. But I had to do it; I wouldn't be able to live with myself if I didn't at least give it a try.

Around four o' clock Randy and I sat down in the living room to make an outline of what we would say. We were deciding on how much money to offer when Suzanne came racing down the stairs.

"Quick! Turn on the TV!" she said breathlessly. "A local station has a news update on Sara!"

Randy took the remote and flipped through the channels until we saw a reporter standing in front of a beach house.

It was Drew's. My heart pounded against my ribs.

"...just arrived," the reporter said as Randy turned up the volume. "All we know at this time is another body has been discovered at this residence. According to police, it's a teenage girl, found shot to death in a small storage room underneath the house."

A cold sweat chilled me.

The reporter continued, "Police say they found no one at the house, which is a rental. However it is currently leased, so we are assuming that whoever is renting it will become the prime suspect in this case that seems to get more bizarre and tragic with each passing day."

chapter 28

I FLED TO my bedroom and locked the door.

I had to be alone. I needed to think.

Was the girl they found Sara? And why did they find the body inside Drew's storage room? And why did the reporter say his house was a rental? Didn't Drew tell me he'd bought it?

Was it a lie?

And if he'd lied about that, how many other things had he lied about?

I fell across the bed and stared up at the ceiling, trying to make sense of it all.

"A.J.?" Randy knocked at the door. "What's going on? Why'd you run in there?"

Drew isn't a killer, I told myself. It's preposterous to think that he could be. Someone must have put that body there. Maybe they saw his picture in the paper and were trying to frame him. He's probably at work and doesn't even know this is happening. Perhaps I should call him.

"A.J? Are you all right?" Randy called out from the other side of the door.

Randy. He didn't know the house they'd shown on TV was Drew's. How was he going to react when he found out?

More banging on the door. "A.J., I know you're upset about them finding the girl, but you shouldn't lock yourself away like this. Open up so we can talk."

I pulled myself from the bed. "I'll open it if you promise me you won't freak out when I tell you something," I said.

"Okay, I promise."

I unlatched the door and let him in.

"God, you look like you've seen a ghost," he said. "And you're shaking."

I choked back my tears. "Randy, I don't understand this, but the house they found the girl at…it belongs to Drew."

He seemed confused at first. Then a look of shock spread across his face. "Jesus, you mean that guy you hooked up with?"

I nodded. "Yes. It doesn't make sense. I know he wouldn't hurt anyone—especially a young girl."

He squeezed his eyelids closed. "Good God, A.J., what have you done? This guy's probably a sociopath and you don't even know it. You probably led him straight to Sara."

"No! He's a doctor! He helps people, he doesn't hurt them!"

"Then why is there a dead girl in his storage room?"

I covered my face with my hands. "I don't know. I don't know anything. But something's all wrong about this. I think he's being set up."

"For your sake, you better be right." He started for the door. "But if you're wrong and he's got something to do with Sara's disappearance, then…"

He didn't finish.

He didn't have to, I could tell by his tone of voice what he was thinking—

He would hold me personally responsible for exposing our daughter to a killer.

chapter 29

THE SUN WENT down, and still we hadn't heard a word from Chief Bowers.

I was beginning to think the man had a sadistic streak; that he enjoyed torturing us by keeping us in suspense, not letting us know if the latest body found was Sara's or not.

Of course the turn of events resulted in us canceling the press conference. We decided it was better to wait and see how things turned out first. Besides, my thoughts were so jumbled and incoherent that I probably wouldn't have made sense anyway.

So now all we could do was wait.

To pass the time, the three of us watched TV, hoping to glean some information about the newly discovered body from the local news stations. But there were no updates. Apparently the police were keeping reporters as much in the dark as they were us.

While we watched an old *Andy Griffith Show* rerun, I asked Randy if he thought I should call Drew. He said absolutely not, that he was probably already in custody and that I should let the police handle him.

I went back to gazing at the TV blankly, paying no attention to the show, lost in my worried thoughts.

Then my cell phone rang.

I took it from the pocket of my shorts. "Unknown" displayed on the caller ID.

With a ragged breath I pushed the connect button.

"A.J., it's me," Drew said, calmly and steadily. "We need to talk."

"Where are you?" I asked.

"That's not important. You know about the girl they found, right?"

"Yes, but I don't understand what's going on. Why was she in your storage room?"

By now Randy and Suzanne were practically sitting in my lap so they could eavesdrop.

"A.J., I swear I didn't have anything to do with that. You've got to believe me."

"I do," I said, feeling a sense of relief. "But there's something I don't understand—they said on the news that you're renting the house. Didn't you tell me you bought it?"

There was a pause. Then he simply said, "I lied."

"Why? Why would you do that?"

"Because I wanted to impress you. I'm sorry things turned out this way."

"Have you talked to the police yet?"

He ignored my question and said, "I'm sorry about all this. It wasn't supposed to work out this way. Everything was going along so well until..."

My stomach fluttered. Something was wrong—his tone had changed. He sounded like someone I had never met.

"I don't know what you're talking about," I said. "Will you please tell me what's going on?"

"I want us to be together," he said in a low whisper. "That's all I ever wanted."

Randy and Suzanne's faces reflected what I was thinking: this guy is about to come unglued.

"Drew, I have to admit you're scaring me a little," I said. "It doesn't sound like you—you seem different."

"That's because I'm upset about them screwing things up. But it's okay—we can still be together. I have a plan."

Suzanne whispered, "This guy's going off the deep end. Maybe you should hang up."

I wasn't willing to do that yet. There was something he was holding back. I had to find out what it was.

"Drew, I'm going to ask you this again, and this time please be honest with me—did you have anything to do with that girl they found today?"

There was a long moment of silence before he said, "No. I already told you that. But there is something you should know."

My body went tense. "What? What do you want me to know?"

"I have Sara. She's been with me all along. And if you want her back, you'll do exactly what I say."

chapter 30

Brenda Sykes.

THAT'S THE NAME of the girl they found in the storage room. I'd seen her face on the poster at Bert's—pretty, blonde, and blue-eyed—just like Sara.

Chief Bowers, in his usual dry manner, sat down with us and filled us in on the details: She had been shot in the back of the head, like the other girls. But there was no sign of assault, sexual or otherwise.

Then he changed the subject to Drew.

"I'm afraid he's been lying to you, Ms, Jenkins," he began. "First of all, his last name isn't Langford, it's Williams. And he's not a doctor—he's an insurance salesman from Virginia."

I wasn't surprised. By now it was apparent that everything he'd told me was a lie; a way for him to get closer to Sara. But I couldn't say anything to Chief Bowers about him holding her hostage. Drew had made me promise that I wouldn't say anything to the cops about it, threatening to do something 'bad' to her if I did. He said he would contact me later with instructions on how I could get her back. That was all he'd said before he hung up.

"So if he's from Virginia what's he doing here on Folly Beach?" Randy asked Chief Bowers.

"He rented a house," he replied. "The one we found the girl at. It looks like he signed a lease for it three weeks ago. It was right after he found out that Ms. Jenkins and Sara were planning on vacationing here."

My mouth dropped open. "What are you talking about? How did he find out we were coming here? I kept that a secret from almost everyone."

His answer shocked us all: "Sara told him about it."

"That's crazy!" I protested. "We didn't even know him until he helped us change the tire."

"But Sara did," he said. "She's been talking to him on a regular basis for months."

I thought he must have lost his mind. But then he explained, "She met Drew online. Except she didn't know he was a man. She thought she was talking to a sixteen year-old girl named Kayla. They became friends, and as Kayla gained her trust, Sara began to give her more and more information about herself."

"I can't believe she would so something like that," I said. "We've had several discussions about the Internet and how dangerous it can be. She's too smart to give out personal information to someone she's never met."

Chief Bowers gave me a condescending smile. "We're all guilty of thinking our children are more responsible than they really are, Ms. Jenkins. Trust me, I see it all the time. Kids get in trouble and the first thing their parents say is 'Oh, no, my Johnny could never do something like that.' But they did. It's just hard for them to accept."

Suzanne spoke up. "Well, this ain't Johnny we're talking about. It's a very intelligent girl named Sara. And she wouldn't let some guy con her like that."

"Why not?" I said, surprising everyone. "He conned me. He had me believing he was a doctor. So how can I blame her when I was just as naïve?"

"A con man is exactly what he is," Chief Bowers said with a nod. "He's got quite a history of it. Swindled a few old folks out of their life savings back in Virginia."

Suzanne sighed. "Okay, help me wrap my head around this thing, will ya? First of all, do you think he's the one who killed the girls? And if so, why would he do it if it was Sara he was after all along?"

"This is what we think," Chief Bowers began. "Sara met Drew online, thinking it was Kayla, several months ago. Drew portrayed himself as a like-minded sixteen year old whose parents had recently divorced—something Sara could immediately identify with. We don't think he knew in the beginning that Sara was the daughter of celebrities—it was just pure chance that they connected in a chat room—but as Sara became more familiar with Kayla she began to open up and talk more about her private life. Then things got even more personal as they started to email each other. When Sara found out that her mother was going to take her to Folly Beach for a vacation, she told Kayla about it and complained about being 'forced' to go. Drew was brilliant, in an evil sort of way, and found out everything he needed to know—when she was going, how she was getting here, and how long she would be staying. As soon as he had the facts, he rented the house here at the beach."

"But that doesn't explain why he would kill those girls," Suzanne said.

"We think he simply snapped," Chief Bowers said. "Maybe he got out here and saw so many teenage girls walking around in bikinis that it triggered something in him. You have to remember we're dealing with a very unstable individual."

"I don't see how it's possible," I said. "I was there at his house. I saw no signs of those girls being there. It seems I would have heard something or would have come across something suspicious. I mean, he couldn't have hidden them all in the storage room. Most of those rooms are pretty tiny out here."

"Maybe he hid them somewhere else," Chief Bowers offered. "A vacant house perhaps."

"But I still don't see how he could have taken Sara," I continued. "I wasn't asleep that long. There's no way he could have snuck out the house, walked down the beach, grabbed her, and hid her in that short amount of time. Plus it seems too coincidental that he happened to find her when she was walking back by herself. I just don't buy it."

Suzanne chipped in, "And how do you know all this stuff about him and Sara talking online? Did you see it on her laptop?"

"Yes, we did," Chief Bowers replied. "And we found emails on his computer at the beach house." He cut his eyes at me. "So, Ms. Jenkins, aren't you glad you came clean with me about him? If I hadn't gone down there to talk with him we would have never found the girl and discovered he was behind all this. I just wish you would have told me about him sooner. Maybe we could have saved that girl. Maybe we could have found Sara by now."

"You son of a bitch!" Randy cried out. "Don't you dare lay a guilt trip on her like that! She had no idea what was going on. She was simply trying to protect someone she thought was innocent from a media feeding frenzy."

I couldn't believe he was standing up for me like that. But then again that's the way Randy had always been—quick to scold me in private, yet quick to take up for me in public.

"I'm sorry, Ms. Jenkins, I meant no offense," Chief Bowers said. "But since we're on the topic of not keeping secrets, don't you think it's time you let me in on the little phone chat you had with Drew this afternoon?"

All of us at the table showed stunned looks.

"How…how did you know about that?" I stuttered.

"We've been monitoring your phone as a precaution. We thought all along that whoever had Sara might try to make contact with you. We wanted to be ready if they did."

"Is that legal?" Randy asked, his face still flush with anger.

"In this case, yes. And it allowed us to trace Drew's phone."

"So you know where he is?" Suzanne asked excitedly.

"Yes and no. We know the call came from the North Charleston area. Unfortunately, he didn't stay on long enough for us to pinpoint him. And as soon as he finished, he turned his phone off. Apparently he knows that it can be traced as long as it's powered up."

"But he warned me not tell you about the call," I said, feeling my stomach curl into a knot. "He said he would do something bad to Sara if I did. What if he finds out you heard everything?"

"He won't. But we want to be here next time he calls. We'd like to silently guide you through the conversation."

"We?" Randy asked. "Who's *we?*"

"Me and the F.B.I. Since we now have a confirmed kidnapping, they will be joining my force on the case. So I hope you don't mind a little company. They'll be camping out here for a while."

My cell phone rang, and I nearly fell out of my chair.

I unhooked it from the belt of my shorts. 'Unknown' displayed on the caller ID.

"It might be him," I told Chief Bowers.

He nodded. "Go ahead and answer it. Put it on speaker phone and try to keep him on as long as you can. They'll be tracing him."

I pushed the connect button and held my breath.

"A.J., it's me," Drew's steady voice crackled through the speaker. "I have to make this quick because I'm sure they're trying to track me. Pack your things and be ready to go tomorrow. I'll tell you where and when so we can make the trade."

"Trade? What trade?" I asked.

"Keep him talking," Chief Bowers whispered. "Come up with something to keep the conversation going."

"I'm talking about the trade we'll make tomorrow," Drew said. "You for Sara. It's what I had planned all along."

He disconnected, leaving us all dumbfounded.

chapter 31

CHIEF BOWERS RETURNED that evening with an FBI agent by the last name of Warren, a dark haired, slender-built man in his thirties. "Agent Warren will be staying here overnight," Chief Bowers informed us. "He's here to guide you through the next phone call Drew makes."

"Please don't let me disturb your normal routine," Agent Warren said. "Just go about your business as if I weren't here."

He had to be kidding. There was nothing about our routine that could be considered normal, not with my daughter being held captive by a sociopathic scumbag.

But we tried to make the best of a bad situation and spent several hours sitting around the living room with Agent Warren, getting to know him and picking his brain on what he thought Drew was up to.

"My take on it is this," he said. "Drew is a con man and a sociopath. He's got the looks and smarts to know how to charm people into whatever he wants, but he has no heart or soul, and he could care less about his victims."

"But why would he kill those girls?" Suzanne asked. "Does he have a history of violence?"

"Not at all," Agent Warren replied. "The only thing we've got on him is a couple of con jobs on elderly people and stalking young girls online. But no violence. So it's puzzling why he turned into a murderer when he got to Folly. Plus, there are a couple of other things that don't seem to fit."

"Like what?" Randy asked.

"Well, none of the victims were sexually assaulted. That's rather unusual in a case like this."

"So why do you think he killed them?" Suzanne asked.

"First of all, let's back up a little. We're making some dangerous assumptions here. We don't know for certain that he killed those girls. Hell, we don't even know for certain that he killed the girl that was found at his house. There's no hard evidence to connect him to the murders other than the fact that we found the one victim in his storage room."

"Yes, there is!" Suzanne exclaimed. "The first girl they found was wearing Sara's shirt. If he had Sara all along, like he says he does, then he must have been the one who murdered her."

"It seems that way," Agent Warren agreed. "But then again, we have to be cautious and not be too quick to jump to conclusions. The only thing we know for sure right now is he claims to have Sara."

"Claims?" I repeated. "You mean you don't believe him?"

"I want proof," he said. "That's something you should ask for when he calls again. Tell him you want to verify that he has Sara before you make any negotiations."

I had a feeling Drew wasn't going to go along with that. After all, he held all the cards. Why would he listen to demands from me?

We chatted a while longer until Agent Warren's cell phone rang. Whoever was on the other end did most of the talking.

After he disconnected, Agent Warren looked straight at me and said, "Ms. Jenkins, I'm afraid I've got some disturbing news."

My heart stuttered in my chest.

"It's not about Sara, so don't be alarmed. It's about Drew."

Thank God, I thought, and let out a relieved breath.

"They just did a thorough investigation of his apartment in Virginia," he explained. "I'm afraid what they found is going to upset you."

"Wait a minute...he still has an apartment in Virginia?" Suzanne asked.

Agent Warren nodded. "Yes, and they found several scrapbooks." Again he looked at me. "They were full of pictures of you, Ms. Jenkins. Apparently Drew is obsessed with you."

"Then why did he take Sara?" I asked. "Why didn't he just take me when he had the chance?"

He shrugged. "Honestly, I don't know. But now it makes sense why he wants to trade her for you. You're the ransom."

"Oh, hell no," Randy cried. "I'm not letting A.J. anywhere near that son of a bitch. So just get that out of your head."

"We would never put Ms. Jenkins in danger. We may pretend to go along with his demands so we can find Sara, but we won't let her get close enough to be in harm's way."

"If it means saving Sara, I'll do it," I said determinedly. "I'll gladly give myself to him if it means she will be safe."

"That's crazy," Randy protested. "All that would do is let him have both of you. You don't really think he's going to give up Sara, do you? We already know he's a lying bastard. What makes you think he's going to honor his end of the deal?"

"I have to agree," Agent Warren said. "Drew is a sociopathic liar. He can't be trusted."

"I can't take any chances on losing Sara, don't you understand that?" I said to both of them. "So if he wants to trade, I'll do it. And I'll be damned if anyone is going to stop me."

Randy and Agent Warren spent the next fifteen minutes trying to convince me otherwise. But I didn't give in; I was ready to sacrifice my life for Sara. What mother wouldn't do the same?

After our tongues grew tired from talking, I warmed up the tuna fish casserole Mrs. Turner had brought over. It wasn't bad, although Agent Warren was the only one who seemed to really enjoy it. In fact, he even had seconds.

It was close to midnight when Agent Warren announced that he was ready to retire for the evening. He asked me where he should crash, and I told him he could use the downstairs guest room, which meant Randy would have to sleep in Sara's room.

We went our separate ways, and before I slipped under the covers I made sure my cell phone had a good charge. Then I placed it on the pillow beside me, just in case Drew called in the middle of the night. As usual, I had a hard time falling asleep, but finally, around two A.M., I managed to doze off.

An hour later, I woke up screaming.

chapter 32

THE NIGHTMARE HAD been about Sara.

She was in a dark, drafty cave. The wind moaned as I felt my way through the winding passageways. Then I heard her call out for me.

"I'm here!" I cried, thrilled to hear her voice. "Tell me where you are so I can find you!"

"I'm right here!" she hollered, her voice echoing off the walls.

"Where? I can hear you but I can't see you."

"Don't you know how close I am, Mom? You can almost touch me! Keep looking!"

Something dropped from the cave's ceiling and landed in front of me with a thud. Like magic, a flashlight appeared in my hand. I turned it on and illuminated the path ahead of me.

It was a corpse. A stinking corpse with maggots crawling all over its decomposing skin.

I dropped the flashlight and screamed.

And now here I was, sitting up in bed, wondering what it all meant.

"A.J., can I come in?" Randy asked from the other side of the door.

"Yes, it's unlocked," I called out.

He opened the door, flicked on the light, and padded across the floor barefoot, wearing gray sweatpants and a sleeveless T-shirt. "You were screaming. I heard you all the way upstairs. Did you have a bad dream?"

I nodded. "Yeah. About Sara."

He eased himself down on the side of the bed. "I've been having nightmares too. I guess everything is playing on our minds while we sleep, huh?"

"This one seemed so real," I said, pulling the covers up to my neck. "I was so close to finding her, but she was in a dark cave and I couldn't see. And then this...this..." I couldn't bring myself to tell him about the corpse.

"It's okay. Like I said, it's just your mind playing tricks on you while you sleep. It's perfectly normal."

Thunder rolled in the distance. I felt a familiar apprehension rise from the depths of my soul and threaten to paralyze me.

"I know how much you hate thunder," Randy said. "It still brings back bad memories of Hugo, doesn't it?"

"My new shrink calls it a trigger," I said. "It's a fancy psychological term for anything that gets my Post Traumatic Stress Disorder kicked into high gear. He gave me some valium to take during thunderstorms, but I've never done it. I don't want to take a chance on getting hooked on that stuff."

A flash of lightning illuminated the room, followed by a clap of thunder, this one louder than the one before. My body jerked in response and my palms went clammy.

"You remember how you used to cuddle up next to me during a storm?" Randy said with a playful grin. "I'd hold you close until it was over. That always seemed to help."

I raised a brow. "Are you making a suggestion?"

Another crack of thunder rattled the window.

"Maybe," Randy said, still smiling. "We're both having trouble sleeping, so why don't we keep each other company?"

Another flash of lightning helped to make up my mind.

"Okay, you can stay," I told him. "But no physical contact—if you try to touch me I'll make you leave."

He laughed. "Yes ma'am. Whatever you say."

"And keep the light on," I added. "I don't want it dark in here during the—"

As luck would have it, the light flickered off.

"Crap," I said, pulling the covers over my head. "I hate it when that happens."

"The lights always go out in a storm on Folly," Randy said. "Shouldn't surprise you."

We were quiet until I broke the silence by saying, "I hate knowing Sara's out there in this storm. Do you think she's all right? You don't think Drew will hurt her, do you?"

"I'm sure she's fine," Randy assured me. "She knows how to take care of herself. She's smart too. She'll know the right things to say to him to keep herself safe."

"I love her so much, Randy. I don't think I'll be able to make it if anything bad happens to her. If it does, you might as well bury me next to her."

"Stop saying things like that. We're going to get her back come hell or highwater. I'm not losing my daughter."

"She worships the ground you walk on. You know that, don't you? I wish she cared as much about me as she does you."

"Are you crazy? That girl thinks the world of you, A.J. She may not always show it, but she respects the hell out of you. I think she wants to follow in your footsteps and be a singer-songwriter."

"She hasn't touched the guitar in months. Except for the other day—I caught her playing in her room. But she doesn't seem to be interested in music anymore. It's like she's shunned it."

"You could have fooled me. Everytime she stays with me she shows me the latest songs she's written."

I pulled the covers down and peered at the shadowy image of his face in the dark. "Since when did she start writing songs?"

"Since a long time ago. Don't tell me she never showed them to you?"

I couldn't believe it. Sara had never mentioned anything to me about writing songs. If she had, I would have been ecstatic and offered to help to her. Why would she keep it a secret from me?

I told Randy this, and he said, "Maybe she didn't think her songs were good enough. I mean, you're such an accomplished songwriter. Maybe she felt she couldn't live up to your standards. But I'm telling you, the ones she sang for me were awesome. The girl's got talent—just like her momma."

I smiled. But it was a fleeting smile, one that vanished as soon as the weight of her situation reentered my thoughts.

A flash of lightning let Randy see the tears pooling in my eyes.

"C'mon, let me hold you," he whispered. "You're upset."

"No," I sobbed. "I don't want you to."

"Yes, you do. You can't fool me."

A bolt of lightning struck so close that I nearly jumped out of my skin.

"Sure you don't want me to hold you?" he asked again. "The storm's getting pretty bad."

"Okay," I surrendered. "But just hold me. Nothing sexual. If I feel anything wiggly down there I'm going to assume it's a snake and chop its head off. Got it?"

He chuckled. "Got it."

I rolled on my side to face away from him. He snuggled next to me and draped his arm around my waist.

"I really miss this," he whispered.

"And whose fault is it that you don't get to do it anymore?" I said.

"Mine. I take all the blame. But I can change, baby, I swear I can. I'll go to therapy—anything you want if you'll give me another chance to prove my love to you."

"Forget it. I could never trust you, Randy. You've never been able to play by the rules when it comes to marriage. I don't think it's in your genes to be faithful."

"You're wrong. Especially now that I've had time to realize what I've lost. You're the only woman I'll ever love, A.J. Those stupid romps in the sack I had with those groupies didn't mean a thing. Hell, I don't even remember their names."

"You're not making things better by telling me that, Randy, so just shut up."

"But I'm trying to get you to see that they were nothing more than a piece of ass. I mean, they literally threw themselves at me. And you know how it is on the road—I was lonely and drunk."

I sighed. "Gee, it's funny how many times I was lonely and drunk, but I never slept with anyone else. Not that I didn't have plenty of chances to do it. But I took our wedding vows seriously, unlike you. So don't give me that 'piece of ass' crap. If you were willing to jeopardize our marriage for a little nookie, then you got what you deserved."

"But I'm a rock star. Girls—"

"Shut up and go to sleep. I've had enough of you."

We lay there for the next several hours, listening to the fading storm, both of us unable to calm our minds enough for sleep. When at last I drifted off, I had another dream about Sara being in a cave. But this one was different because my mother was there and I heard chimes; beautiful, haunting chimes that played a melody so familiar, yet I couldn't recall its name.

I woke up with the feeling that it meant something important, although I had no idea what it could be.

chapter 33

MRS. GAYLORD—SUZANNE'S much tooted psychic—arrived shortly after ten AM.

She entered with a flourish, giving Suzanne a kiss on the cheek, then embracing me with open arms. "Oh, you poor dear," she whispered close to my ear. "I know how much pain losing Sara has caused you. But I've been assured by The Spirits that she is alive and in good health."

I judged her as being in her seventies, slightly bent from osteoporosis, yet full of energy. And her eyes—God, they were so blue and clear, giving the impression that she was a young woman trapped inside an age-worn body.

"Thank you for coming, Mrs. Gaylord," I said as she clasped my hands between hers. "Suzanne has told me a lot of good things about you."

She didn't respond. Instead, she squeezed her eyelids together and became silent.

"Mrs. Gaylord? Is something wrong?" I asked.

She shook her head slowly, keeping her eyelids pressed firmly together. "No, dear, I'm receiving a message from The Spirits. They're telling me that you are no stranger to tragedy, and neither is this house. They say there are several souls gathered here; one who appears to be a mother figure. They say she's been reaching out for you."

"Do...do you think it's my mother?" I asked, feeling goosebumps sprout on my arms and legs.

"Very likely. The Spirits tell me that she remains close to this place. And they're showing me a silver cord, which is symbolic of a mother-child relationship. And they say she is trying to tell them something...something about a..." Her eyes flew open. With a frown, she said, "Damn, they're gone. Something must have spooked them."

I wanted to ask her how spirits could get spooked, but before I had a chance to speak she said, "Take me to Sara's room. It will be most helpful if I can touch some of her things, especially her clothes and jewelry."

Suzanne tagged along as Mrs. Gaylord followed me upstairs. As soon as I opened the door to Sara's room, she began to tell me things about my daughter's 'vibration.'

"She's a soul with many gifts," Mrs. Gaylord said. "Especially when it comes to music. And very intuitive—she can feel and see things most people can't." She crossed the room to Sara's closet and opened it. Pulling a sundress off its hanger, she added, "There's something special about this child; God has great plans for her. But for now I fear she is in grave danger." She brought the sundress to her bosom and held it close. "She is being kept by someone evil; someone who has lost touch with reality."

"We already know that," Suzanne said. "We even know who it is. But we don't know where he's keeping her. Can you ask your spirit friends to check into that for us?"

Once again she closed her eyes. After a moment of silence, she said, "The Spirits are showing me a dark place, like a heavily wooded oak forest—a place where sunlight is blocked by a canopy of leaves. And there's a strong wind blowing—I hear chimes clanging in the stiff breeze."

I sucked in my breath. "Chimes? I had a dream about chimes just this morning. Do you think they're the same ones?"

Mrs. Gaylord opened her eyes and smiled. "Yes. The Sprits told me the wind will lead you to Sara."

"Oh, great," Suzanne said with a sigh. "That really tells us a lot. What are we supposed to do? Release a balloon and see where the wind takes it?"

Mrs. Gaylord put the sundress back on its hanger. She shook her head and said, "Suzanne, Suzanne. How many years have you been coming to see me?"

Suzanne shrugged. "About three, I guess."

"And how many times have I told you that The Spirits speak symbolically? There's a deeper meaning hidden in their message. It's up to us to figure out what it is."

"Well, why can't they just come out and say what they've got to say?" Suzanne wanted to know. "Like that time they told you I was going to get that movie role I was after."

Mrs. Gaylord was about to answer, but was interrupted by my cell phone ringing.

I reached into the pocket of my cargo shorts and pulled it out. The caller ID displayed 'Unknown.'

"Oh, God, it must be Drew," I gasped.

"I'll get Agent Warren," Suzanne said.

I took a deep breath and pushed the connect button.

chapter 34

"HELLO, SUNSHINE," DREW began in a relaxed voice. "Did you sleep well last night?"

Anger and frustration rose in my throat, begging for release, begging for me to tell him to go to hell. But there was too much at stake to allow myself that luxury. I had to concentrate on the task at hand: keeping him on the phone long enough for the FBI to track his call.

"No, I didn't sleep well at all," I said through quivering lips. "I'm worried about Sara, Drew. Is she all right? Can I talk to her?"

"She's a little tied up right now," he said with a laugh. "But she's fine. Except I can't get her to eat. I even made her an omelet for breakfast, but she turned that cute little nose of hers up at it."

Randy and Agent Warren came rushing into the room. "Is it him?" Agent Warren mouthed.

I nodded.

He motioned for me to turn the phone's speaker on.

I pushed the button just in time for him to hear Drew say, "Have you packed you bags? Today's our big day, you know? We can finally be together forever."

"I'll do anything you want," I said. "But please let Sara go. She's just a kid, Drew. She has her whole life ahead of her."

"Of course, I'll let her go...as long you follow my plan. It's as simple as that."

"And what exactly is this plan?" I asked.

"I want to take you to a special place...a place I've prepared for you and me; a place where we can make love for the rest of our lives."

I cringed at the thought. "And what about Sara? Are you going to release her if I go along with this?"

"Yes. As long as the police don't interfere."

"How do I know you're telling the truth?" I asked. "How do I know you won't keep us both hostage?"

"What do you mean by *hostage?*" His voice turned edgy. "Don't you *want* to be with me?"

I reminded myself that I was talking to an unstable man; one who might snap and do harm to Sara if I didn't say the right thing.

"Yes, I want to be with you," I lied. "But before I commit to your plan I want you to prove to me that Sara's okay."

He paused. "The police are there, aren't they?"

I looked at Agent Warren. He nodded and told me to say yes.

"There's an FBI agent with me," I admitted.

"I knew there would be," Drew said smugly. "I watch TV so I know how these things work. I was testing you to see if you would tell me the truth. And I'm sure he's the one who's making you ask me for proof that I have Sara. They always do that—all you have to do is watch a few kidnapping movies to know that. So listen up Mr. FBI man, I know you're listening and I've got something to tell you that will leave no doubt that I have her.

Just have your boys take a look at the deck on the back of my house. They should find a loose floorboard. Taped to the bottom of it is a necklace with a heart-shaped pendent. I think you know who it belongs to, don't you, A.J.?"

I raised my hand to my mouth. "Oh, my God, it's the one Sara was wearing when she met us at the pier."

"Exactly. It has a beautiful blue sapphire in the center that matches the color of her eyes. I believe it's her birthstone, isn't it?"

"That son of a bitch," Randy snarled. "That's the pendent we gave her for her birthday."

"Anyway," Drew continued, "I put it there because I knew this proof thing would come up. So go find the necklace, and I'll call you back in a little while with instructions on where to meet me. But remember—if I see one cop or FBI agent, or if I find a wire or some other tracking device on you, it's all over for Sara. I'm the only one who knows where she is, and if my plan gets foiled I'll never tell a soul where I've hidden her. She'll die a slow, agonizing death from a lack of oxygen. You don't want that to happen, do you, A.J.?"

"No," I said, sniffling back my tears. "I'll do anything you want as long as you don't hurt her."

"Good. I'll talk to you later."

He disconnected. Agent Warren smiled at me and said, "You did good. He was on there for quite a while. They should be able to pinpoint his location."

"I hope so," I said as Randy gathered me into his arms. "For Sara's sake, I hope so."

chapter 35

DREW WAS SMARTER than any of us had imagined. His cell phone signal had come from a wooded area near Bowman, a rural community between Charleston and Columbia. The FBI theorized that he'd driven to the edge of the woods, hiked a good ways in, then made the call. Of course he turned the phone off as soon as he finished, which made it impossible to know which way he went afterwards. So in essence we were no closer to finding him or Sara than we were before the call was made.

"Do you think he could be staying in the woods?" Randy asked Agent Warren after he gave us the bad news. "Maybe that's where he's keeping Sara."

"We don't think so," he said. "They found tire tracks on the dirt road that are consistent with the type of vehicle he's driving. They indicate he took the road back to the main highway after the call. Where he went after that is anybody's guess."

"Mrs. Gaylord said she had a vision about woods," Suzanne pointed out. "With lots of oak trees. So maybe that means Sara is close to where he made the call."

Mrs. Gaylord had been quiet until now. She shook her head and said, "Something doesn't seem right. I definitely saw the woods, but I'm not feeling an association between that man and Sara. Of course, The Spirits aren't always right—they only have a seventy percent accuracy rating. But I can't shake the feeling that there's more to this than we know."

"Well, why don't you ask The Spirits to elaborate?" Suzanne suggested. "Tell them this is important shit and not to screw it up."

Mrs. Gaylord shook her head. "My dear, sweet Suzanne, must you always be so blunt? And don't you know by now that The Spirits don't respond well to me pressuring them? If there's more they want us to know, I'm sure they'll..." her voice trailed off and she stared straight ahead.

"Mrs. Gaylord? Are you okay?" I asked.

She didn't say anything.

"I bet The Spirits are talking to her," Suzanne said. "She might be in a trance."

Randy rolled his eyes. "You guys don't really believe in this nonsense, do you? I can't believe you're wasting your time with this quack."

"She's not a quack," Suzanne fired back. "She's Hollywood's most respected psychic. She predicted the big earthquake we had last year and the Malibu fires. And she's gotten a bunch of crap about me right. So stop being so judgmental and—"

"Dolphins," Mrs. Gaylord said, her eyes closed now. "The Spirits are showing me dolphins. Three of them. They are very close to Sara. Blue dolphins."

"Great," Randy snickered. "So what does that mean? Sara's on a deserted island somewhere?"

Mrs. Gaylord opened her eyes. "They are gone now. But the dolphins mean something important. Of that, I'm certain."

Randy sighed. "First woods, now dolphins. Damn, we don't know whether to look for her on land or water. Some help you are."

"Stop being so rude," I snapped. "She can't help what she sees. Maybe it doesn't make sense now but it might mean something in the future. So shut up and keep your comments to yourself."

He pointed a finger at me. "Don't tell me to shut up. If you hadn't screwed around with that guy none of this would have happened in the first place."

I lurched at him, my hand raised to slap his cheek. Fortunately for him, Suzanne stood between us just in time to stop me.

"Are ya'll crazy?" she said, her eyes darting between the two of us. "Your daughter's life is in jeopardy and you're acting like a couple of kindergartners. I know the stress is wearing thin on all of us, but we've got to stay united."

"Well put, Suzanne," Mrs. Gaylord said.

"I'm still not happy about you inviting this charlatan into our house," Randy sneered. "But if you want to live in a fantasy world, go right ahead."

I crossed my arms. "It's *my* house now, remember? You lost your share of it with the divorce. So I can invite anyone I please."

"Guys! Stop!" Suzanne cried. "You're doing it again!"

"She's right, folks," Agent Warren said. "We don't have time to waste on bickering. Drew could call again at any moment and we have to be prepared."

"What if he insists on trading Sara for A.J.?" Randy asked. "There's no way I'm going to let that happen."

I narrowed my eyes at him. "Oh, really? Just five seconds ago you were ready to kill me. Now you want to protect me?"

"Don't be ridiculous," he said. "You know how much I care about you. And I'm not going to let you put yourself in harm's way."

"I'll do whatever I damn well please," I shot back. "Especially if it saves our daughter's life."

Agent Warren raised his hands. "Folks, please stop. They're working on a plan right now that will keep Ms. Jenkins out of danger."

"And how do you propose to do that?" Randy asked.

"I'm not sure yet, but they may send a look-alike to the meet so we can nail this guy."

I looked at him with a shocked expression. "A look-alike? Are you out of your mind? Didn't you hear anything Drew said? If he doesn't get me he's not going to tell you where Sara is."

"All that's being worked out," Agent Warren said.

"How?" I demanded. "This is my daughter's life we're talking about. We can't take a chance on doing something wrong."

"We also can't take a chance on Drew taking you hostage," Agent Warren said. "Odds are good that he has no intention of letting Sara go, even if you follow his so-called plan exactly. You have to keep in mind that he's a pathological liar, a con man. He'll tell you anything you want to hear so he can get what he wants."

"Exactly," Randy chipped in. "That's why we need to figure out a way to make him give up Sara first."

"Good luck with that," Mrs. Gaylord said. "You're dealing with the devil himself with that man. He's possessed, yet he's got a brilliant mind. The demon inside him is using it to his advantage."

"Oh, God, not the demon thing," Randy said, giving her another eye roll. "Maybe we ought to call an exorcist for him."

Mrs. Gaylord smiled. "Son, you have a few demons yourself. One of them caused your wife to divorce you. So I'd worry about getting yours under control before you worry about other people."

Randy gave her a dirty stare but didn't say anything.

Just then, Agent Warren's cell phone rang. He listened to the person on the other end without saying much, just a few 'uh-huhs' now and then. When he finished, he frowned and said, "They found the pendent where Drew told us it was." He hesitated, avoiding my gaze. "There's something else you should know. They found blood on the chain."

I sank to my knees, wondering how much more of this I could take.

chapter 36

It was noon when Drew called again.

He got right down to business by asking, "Did they find the pendent?"

"Yes, it was right where you said it would be," I told him.

"So that should prove to you that I have Sara."

I sat down on the sofa, trying to contain my anger. "Drew, they found blood on the chain. Is it Sara's?"

There was a long pause before he said, "No. Sara's fine. I haven't hurt her in any way."

Agent Warren and Randy seated themselves on opposite sides of me. "Ask him how the blood got there," Agent Warren whispered into my ear.

"So how do you explain the blood being on her necklace?" I said. "If it isn't hers, whose is it?"

He paused again. "It's the girl's blood—the one they found in the storage room. I must have handled the necklace after I killed her."

Agent Warren and I exchanged surprised looks. "I...I thought you said you didn't kill that girl? Does that mean you killed the other girls too?"

"I don't want to talk about that!" His voice became harsh and loud. "You're trying to distract me; trying to keep me on the phone longer so they can locate me. But they'll never find me. And they'll never find Sara unless I tell them where she is. So you better do as I say!"

"I will," I assured him. "But if we're going to spend the rest of our lives together, don't you think you owe it to me to explain your actions? Don't you think I should know why you killed those girls?"

"We'll have plenty of time to discuss that once we're together. Have you packed your bags?"

I swallowed hard. "Yes, they're packed. What do you want me to do?"

"I'm going to give you the address of an abandoned house in Charleston. Meet me there at two o'clock sharp. No police, no FBI. I will strip search you for wires, so I better not find any. Then we'll get in my car and go to the place I've prepared for us. If everything goes okay and I know for sure we weren't followed, I'll send a message to the police letting them know where they can find Sara. It's as simple as that."

Agent Warren whispered, "Tell him you'll go through with it if he lets you talk to Sara first. Be firm."

I nodded. "Drew, please let me talk to Sara. That's all I ask. If you do, I'll meet you at two o'clock. I promise I will."

"Godammit, you're not the one setting the rules!" he exploded. "You want Sara to live? Then you'll do what I say! If not, I'll shoot her in the back of the head, just like the other girls!"

It was clear that he wasn't going to negotiate. I had no choice but to say, "Okay, we'll do everything your way. Where do you want to meet me?"

"That's my girl," he said in a calmer tone. "Stop listening to the FBI and everything will be just fine. I'll call you at one-thirty and tell you where the house is. But make sure you come alone. I'm not joking about killing Sara if you—"

I siren wailed over the phone's speaker. A mortified look spread across Agent Warren's face.

"Shit!" Drew cried. "I told you no cops, didn't I? So why is there a goddam highway patrolman on my ass?"

"No one is supposed to stop him," Agent Warren said. "This shouldn't be happening."

"He's chasing me! The frickin' cop is chasing me!" Drew yelled. "You better get him to back off if you want Sara to live!"

Agent Warren frantically punched numbers into his cell phone. "I'm calling the highway patrol office right now. I'll tell them to stop the pursuit," he said.

"Drew, we're going to get him to stop," I relayed. "And I swear we didn't have anything to do with this. It must be a mistake."

"Mistake my ass! The bastard won't get off my tail. If he catches me it will be all over for Sara. There's not much air left where I hid her. And I won't tell anyone where that is. So she's going to suffocate, A.J. You hear me? She's going to suffocate because you didn't listen to me and play by my rules!"

"Drew, please! We're going to get him to stop. I swear, we are!"

"Lying bitch! I thought I could trust you. But you're just like all the others, aren't you? I should have put a bullet in your head when I had the chance. But I thought you were different—I thought we had something special; something magical. I really loved you, A.J. Too bad you had to screw it all up. Too bad Sara has to die because of it."

"She has nothing to do with this!" My chest heaved and I burst into sobs. "Please tell me where she is and stop this insanity!"

I heard the sound of brakes squealing, followed by a gut-wrenching scream.

Then there was silence.

"Drew? Are you there?" I asked, although I knew we had been disconnected.

"What the hell just happened?" Agent Warren barked into his cell. "It sounded like our guy just wrecked!"

"Drew?" I repeated, zombielike, unable to put the phone down. If something bad had happened to him it was all over. Sara would die from suffocation before anyone could find her.

Randy pried the phone from my hand and put his arm around me. "It's going to be okay, baby," he said softly.

I buried my face into his chest. "She's going to die, isn't she?"

"No, nothing's going to happen to her. We'll find her, no matter what."

I took little comfort in his empty promise, yet I didn't have the strength to argue. I was close to the edge now; a breath away from falling into the dark, bottomless pit my life would become without Sara.

Agent Warren murmured a few things into his phone, then clicked it off.

"Well?" Randy asked. "What did you find out?"

The long sigh he gave confirmed my fear—Drew was gone.

"He lost control of his car," Agent Warren said. "He went down an embankment and hit a tree head-on. I'm afraid he perished upon impact."

"Godammit!" Randy cried. "How did this happen? Why did that trooper try to stop him?"

"Miscommunication," Agent Warren said. "The trooper knew there was a BOLO for the car but didn't know there was a standing order not to stop it. He should have just reported that he had it in sight and let us do the rest."

"And now Sara's going to die," I bawled.

"We're not going to let that happen, Ms. Jenkins," Agent Warren assured me. "We're already canvassing the area he called from yesterday. We have a hunch he hid Sara somewhere in that vicinity. Plus, there's a good chance he left some evidence in the car that might help us locate her."

I raised my head from Randy's chest and looked across the room at Mrs. Gaylord. "Please help us," I begged. "You're our only hope now. Please tell us where she is before it's too late."

She smiled sadly. "I'll try, dear. But I can't force these things." She approached me with her hand extended. I took it and she helped me to my feet. Gazing directly into my eyes, she said, "You're the mother. No one is as close to that child's spirit as you are. Trust your intuition; it will guide you to her if you allow it to."

Could that be possible? I wondered, remembering the dream I had. If that was my 'intuition' at work, it was pretty meaningless. A cave and some chimes. This was the Lowcountry; there were no caves around here. And the chimes? What was I supposed to do about that? Have the FBI check out every house that had them hanging in their backyard?

Yet I couldn't shake the feeling that Sara had been calling out to me in that dream. And she had seemed so close, not far away in some wooded area. Maybe it meant Drew had hidden her somewhere on the beach. That would be more consistent with the dolphins Mrs. Gaylord had seen, and—

"What are you thinking?" Mrs. Gaylord asked me.

I shook my head. "Nothing. I was just mulling things over, that's all."

She touched my cheek. "Intuition. It's the most powerful gift God gave Women. Put it to good use." Her eyes danced and smiled.

Then she walked away.

chapter 37

SINCE THERE WAS nothing more he could do at the house, Agent Warren excused himself and went to his office to 'follow up on things.' He took Mrs. Gaylord along, promising her that he would drive her out to the wooded area in Bowman that had become the focal point in the search for Sara. That left me, Randy, and Suzanne to sit around and worry about Sara's fate while precious moments ticked away—moments that could mean the difference between finding her alive or finding her dead.

At five o'clock Agent Warren called to tell us that the searchers had found nothing so far. He informed us that authorities were in the process of going to the farm houses and mobile homes that dotted the rural landscape and asking people if they had seen anything suspicious. They were also entering vacant houses and barns, since those were considered to be the most likely places where Drew would have hid Sara. But out of the several they had come across, none showed signs that they had been occupied recently. So they were expanding the search and hoping against hope that Mrs. Gaylord might 'sense' something.

I, on the other hand, couldn't shake the feeling that they were on a wild goose chase; that Drew had hidden Sara somewhere much closer, perhaps at Folly. I even called Chief Bowers and asked him if he would consider checking out all the vacant houses on the beach. He responded by telling me that he would give it some thought. I could tell by the tone of his voice that it would never happen.

As the sun sank lower, our moods became as dark and heavy as the gathering thunderclouds just offshore. If Drew had indeed left Sara with 'very little air,' her time was rapidly running out. I couldn't help but visualize her gasping for oxygen, clawing at whatever enclosure Drew had put her in. And there were the inevitable images of her funeral; flashes of her lying in a coffin, her skin pale and her lips blue. I willed them to go away but they kept returning; kept haunting me over and over, until I was so frazzled that I could barely manage to function.

Suzanne and Randy were hurting too. I could tell, despite their gallant efforts to disguise it for my sake. They kept assuring me that everything would be okay; empty words that people use when they have nothing else to offer you. I was growing tired of empty words and empty promises. But they kept coming, like sympathy cards offered in advance of a tragedy. They no longer soothed me, only irritated me. How could everything be okay? My daughter could be dying and there wasn't a damn thing I could do about it. And it was all my fault—I was the one stupid enough to fall for Drew. I was the one stupid enough to bring Sara right to him. If anything happened to her, I deserved to die too. In fact, I would make sure of it.

As twilight fell, Suzanne let us know that she was having menstrual cramps and wanted to lie down for a while. After she went upstairs, Randy sat on the sofa and silently held me until he began to snore. I moved his arm away and padded off to the kitchen.

I had to do something to keep from going insane, so I washed the dishes by hand. There weren't many of them—we hadn't eaten much in the past few days—so it didn't take long for me to get to the last item in the sink: the casserole dish Mrs. Turner had brought over.

I had no idea why, but I found myself staring at it. Then a thought hit me: *I could take it back to her.*

It would be so nice to get out of the house, just for a few moments. And with Randy and Suzanne both napping, it was the perfect opportunity to do so without them stopping me. Of course I knew the media and paparazzi were lurking just outside, but if I snuck out the back door and took the path that ran along the dunes to her house, there was a good chance they wouldn't see me. And, Lord, how wonderful it would be to breathe in the salty air instead of the stale, stagnant air that had been circulating in the house since we had to close it up. Maybe it would clear my head. Maybe I could think better afterwards.

Then I remembered—a security guard was supposed to be watching the beach side of the house to keep reporters or curiosity seekers from getting too close. What would he do if he saw me? Order me back inside?

The hell with it, I thought. *This is my house and I'll do as I damn well please. I'm tired of being a prisoner in it. I'm going, no matter what.*

I dried the dish and stole out the French doors.

There was no security guard outside. Maybe he was on a break or something. If he was, I wasn't complaining.

I sprinted along the sandy path on the lee side of the dunes, nervously scanning my surroundings in the fading daylight like a prisoner escaping from a penitentiary.

I was just about to reach the stairs leading to Mrs. Turner's screen porch when I heard her call out my name.

It startled me so much that I almost dropped the dish.

"You scared me," I said, catching my breath.

She approached me, holding a pair of garden clippers. "I didn't mean to, honey," she said with a laugh. "I was just trying to get some last minute things done out here before it gets too dark. Plus, I like to work outside this time of day, since it ain't so damn hot." She spied the dish I was holding. "You bringing that back to me?"

I nodded. "Yeah, I needed to get out of the house for a few minutes and this gave me a good excuse to do it." I held it out for her to take. "Thanks for making us the casserole. That was very thoughtful of you."

She set the clippers down and took the dish. "It was my pleasure, sweetie. It was the least I could do for you." A tear formed in her eye. "I'm so sorry about everything, honey. I've been listening to the news and heard what happened to that jackass who hid Sara. Are they getting any closer to finding her?"

"No," I said. "It's anyone's guess where she is. They think she might be in a wooded area near Bowman, but I think…" I shook my head. "Never mind. I'm probably wrong."

"Wrong about what, honey?"

I took in a deep breath of the ocean air and let it out slowly. "I just have this nagging feeling that she's here on the beach somewhere."

"Mother's intuition," Mrs. Turner said with a crooked smile. "It ain't nothin' to play around with, from what I've heard."

"You're the second person to say something like that to me today," I said, forcing a smile in return. "But I'm afraid no one is taking me seriously."

"I take you seriously, sweetie. I believe in stuff like that."
She nodded toward the stairs. "You want to come up and sit on
the porch for a while? It might do you good."

I shook my head. "No, thanks. I better not stay long. No
one knows I came over here. If one of them wakes up from their
nap and finds me gone, they might freak."

"They're napping, huh?" Mrs. Turner said. She paused as
if she were lost in thought. "Sure you don't want to stay a few
minutes? We could drink a cold one together."

"No, I better not. But thanks for the offer. And thanks
again for—" A sudden breeze rustled the palmettos. Wind
chimes began to clang.

Their haunting melody sounded so familiar...

"A.J., honey, is something wrong?" Mrs. Turner asked.
"You look a little funny."

I raised my eyes. The chimes were hanging from an eve
above the door to Mrs. Turner's screen porch. Three glass dolphins strung to the mount circled the chimes lazily in the wind.

"Oh, my God," I whispered. "Can it be?"

"Can it be what?" Mrs. Turner asked.

"The chimes. I heard them in a dream. And Mrs. Gaylord
saw three dolphins in her vision."

"Honey, I ain't got no idea what you're talking about."

I turned my eyes to her. "Mrs. Turner, do you know where
Sara is?" I couldn't believe I was asking her that. It seemed ab-
surd that she would have anything to do with her disappearance.
Yet I felt compelled to confront her.

Her lips quivered for a brief second. "Why would you ask
me something like that? Of course, I don't know where she is. If
I did, I'd tell you."

I knew she was lying. I could tell by the way her eyes hardened, by the way the tone of her voice lowered.

"Where is she, Mrs. Turner?" I said firmly. "Tell me where my daughter is."

"Honey, you're talking fool. You need to go back to your house and get some rest. I'm worried about you."

I drew closer to her. "I'm not going anywhere until you tell me what you know."

She took a step back. "Sweetie, I don't want to call the cops. But I will if you don't stop acting like you're possessed."

The wind picked up again. The chimes clanged louder.

"Go home," Mrs. Turner said, starting toward the stairs. "You're delusional from grief. You need a psychiatrist."

"I'm not leaving until I go inside your house." I surprised myself by being so brazen. It was as if someone else were speaking through me; someone stronger and bolder.

"No, you're going home," Mrs. Turner insisted.

I moved toward her. "Let me inside your house or I'll call the police and get them to search it."

She leaned against the rail at the bottom of the steps and laughed. "Oh, really? And on what grounds are they going to get a search warrant? Your crazy dream? I hardly think so."

In a moment of pure impulse I pushed past her and climbed the stairs.

"A.J. you're making a big mistake," she called after me. "You don't want to do this."

I ignored her and scanned the porch for anything unusual. Not finding anything, I entered the living room through an open door.

The walls were dark, made of oak paneling, and the old heart of pine floor creaked with every step I took as I wandered through the sparsely furnished room. Everything was neat and orderly. No signs of Sara or any indication that she had ever been there.

I took a nervous glance over my shoulder and proceeded to the kitchen.

That's where I found something that caused me to suck in my breath.

Sara's MyFi. The one Suzanne had given her.

I clutched it in my hand and held it to my breast.

"Well, well, what have you got there?" Mrs. Turner asked, causing me to jump.

I couldn't speak as she brushed past me on the way to the refrigerator. She opened it and took out a beer. "You want one?" she asked.

I moved my mouth but no words came out.

"Couldn't leave well enough alone, could you?" she said as she twisted the cap off the beer. She took a swallow and added, "You had to go and snoop around. All because of some silly dream. Such a shame." She shook her head and reached into the fridge for another beer. "I'm getting you a cold one whether you like it or not."

"I...I don't understand," I managed to stutter. "Why do you have Sara's WiFi?"

She used her foot to close the refrigerator door. "She doesn't need that damn thing," she said as she walked toward me. "Have you heard the kind of music she was listening to? Disgusting and immoral, that's what it is. Sexually explicit, as they say. You really should have kept a closer eye on that child and monitored what she listened to." She thrust the beer at me. "Take it...you're going to be here for a while, so you might as well relax."

"I don't want it!" I shot back. "I just want you to tell me what's going on!"

She set the bottle down on the counter and went over to a drawer near the sink. "I wish you'd let me do this the easy way," she said as she opened it. "I'm trying to be nice to you, offering you a beer and willing to explain everything, and what do you do? Go and yell at me, that's what you do. So I guess we'll have to do this the hard way." She took a handgun from the drawer and aimed it at me.

For a moment my mind refused to believe what I was seeing. How could Mrs. Turner, one of the sweetest ladies I knew, be threatening me with a gun? But the look in her eyes let me know it was no idle threat.

With my heart pounding against my ribs, I asked, "Why are you doing this? Why would you want to hurt me?"

She nodded toward a small round table in the breakfast nook. "Go sit your ass over there and I'll tell you all about it."

I couldn't get my feet to move.

"You think I'm joking? Have you noticed I'm pointing a fully loaded Beretta at your head? Now get moving!"

I hurried to the nook and took a seat. With the gun in one hand and the bottles of beer in the other, Mrs. Turner kicked a chair out from the table and settled into it. "Drink up," she said, handing me the beer.

I reluctantly took it from her.

"Honey, I really hate that it's come to this," she said. "I really like you a lot. In fact, I love you. But I love Sara even more. That's why I wish you hadn't poked your nose into this."

"Into what, Mrs. Turner? I don't understand what's going on."

She pointed to my beer. "Take a sip, honey. It'll calm your nerves. You're shaking like a leaf."

I brought the bottle to my lips and took a swallow just so I could please her.

"Good girl. That'll calm you. No use in working yourself into a frenzy."

I set the bottle down and gazed at her with pleading eyes. "Please, Mrs. Turner, tell me what's going on. If you know where Sara is, take me to her."

She leaned back in her chair. "You ain't got far to go, honey. Sara's right here with me. I've been taking real good care of her."

I looked at her in disbelief. "What? How can that be? Drew said he had her. Don't tell me you two were in cahoots."

She laughed boisterously. "Are you kidding? Me in cahoots with that idiot?" She shook her head, still chuckling. "Lord, did he ever pull the rug over your eyes. But I've got to hand it to him—he certainly knew how to take advantage of a situation. It was actually quite brilliant of him to get you to think he had Sara."

My blood ran cold. "You mean he never had her? You had her all along?"

She nodded proudly. "And I must say I'm pretty brilliant for framing him. I wonder if he shit his pants when he found that girl in his storage room."

I felt sick to my stomach. "You mean *you* killed that girl?"

"Of course. Just like those other three bitches. They weren't fit to have as a daughter."

"A *daughter*? What the hell are you talking about?"

She took a swig of her beer. "Honey, remember how I told you I couldn't have any children? And remember how I told you that bastard of a husband of mine wouldn't let me adopt one? Well, it left a hole in my soul I could never fill. All I ever wanted was a daughter I could love and raise to be a respectable young lady. But he took that from me." She took another gulp from the bottle. "When I found out I was dying, I decided to do something about it."

"*Dying?* You never told me you were dying."

She shrugged. "Never came up, I suppose. It's a tumor—in the brain. Inoperable. To be quite honest, I think it's making me a little loony."

Loony? The woman was downright *insane*.

"Why'd you do it?" I asked. "Why'd you kill those poor girls?"

She gave me a dismissive wave of her hand. "Those girls were disrespectful. Called me all sorts of names and refused to cooperate. I couldn't see none of them being my daughter, so I disposed of them."

"Disposed of them?" My jaw dropped. "My God, you make it sound like they were garbage. They were human beings, for crying out loud. Young girls whose lives had just started. How could you take that away from them?"

"Oh, cry me a river. They got what they deserved. They're nothing like Sara. She's so well-behaved and polite. She's a daughter I can be proud of."

I wanted to scream, to grab hold of her neck and strangle her. But she had a gun. I couldn't save Sara if I were dead; I had to stay calm and figure out a way to outsmart the bitch.

"So you took Sara so she could be your daughter?" I said, playing along with her sick way of thinking.

She nodded. "Sara is my dream daughter—blonde, beautiful, and intelligent. Those others paled in comparison. It was easy to get rid of them when I got her."

"You should have just let them go."

She snorted. "Yeah, right. And let them run to mommy and daddy and tell them about the crazy old woman who took them? I hardly think so. I might be loony, but I'm not stupid."

"So why did you dress one of the girls in Sara's shirt? Was it some sort of message?"

She smiled. "Naw. I was just playing with you. I did it for the hell of it. Just like the way I put Sara's necklace on the girl I left at Drew's house. I wanted to mess with your head."

So that's how Drew got the necklace, I thought. It made me wonder who was more insane—Mrs. Turner or him.

"But how did you know Drew?" I asked. "Why did you decide to frame him?"

"That crazy hoot was snooping around your house days before you got here," she said. "I got to talking with him one afternoon and asked him why he was nosing around so much. He came up with some lame excuse about being in the market for a house and he'd heard yours was going up for sale. Well, I knew that was a lie 'cause you'd never get rid of that house; I know how much it means to you after losing your family there and all. Anyway, I ran into him one day at Bert's and asked him if he'd bought anything. He told me about the one he rented, except he tried to make it sound like he was buying it. I knew it was another lie—The Grants own that house and they ain't never gonna sell it. So I figured the bastard was up to no good. Then I seen that picture of you and him kissing on the pier, and I seen it on all the TV gossip shows. So I figured he was trying to con you into something. That's why I framed him. I was trying to protect you, A.J. Can't you see that? But I had no idea the crazy old hoot would use the whole thing to his advantage and make you think he had Sara." She laughed. "It's a hell of a world, ain't it? Can't trust no one these days." She looked at my beer. "You ain't drinking, honey. Take a sip so you can loosen up."

I narrowed my eyes at her. "I don't want to loosen up. I want you to stop this insanity right now and give me my daughter!"

"Let's see," she said, pointing the gun at my heart. "I'm the one with the weapon and you're not. Looks like I should be the one giving the orders, not you."

"What are you going to do? Kill me?"

Her lips formed a slight grin. "Oh, Lord, no. Not in here, anyway. I don't want your blood all over my kitchen, especially after I just spent the whole afternoon cleaning it."

I slammed my palms down onto the table. "Look, you stupid bitch, I've had just about all I can take of this! So if you're going to shoot me, shoot me. If not, take me to my daughter!"

She studied me for a moment, as if she were trying to decide which option to go with.

"I admire the hell out of you, girl," she finally said. "Not many women would say something like that to a crazy old lady with a gun. You got balls. Too bad this isn't going to work out well for you."

"What do you mean?"

"I'm gonna have to kill you, honey. I sure as hell can't let you go home and call the cops on me, now can I? And I sure as hell ain't gonna let you have Sara back. She's mine now. I'm keeping her until I croak—which, according to the doctors, ain't gonna be much longer."

"Let me do everyone a favor and end your miserable life for you now," I offered.

She chuckled. "Like I said, you got balls. Too bad the world has to say goodbye to you and your songs. I'm sure you'll be sorely missed by your fans." She waved the gun at me. "Get up. Let's go see your daughter. The least I can do is let you say goodbye to her."

chapter 38

Mrs. Turner walked me down a dark hall, so narrow that it reminded me of the passageway in the cave I had the nightmare about.

"Sara's in the room at the end," she said, poking my back with the gun. "I'm sure she'll be surprised to see you."

She had me turn the knob and open the door.

My heart leaped when I saw Sara. But it sank when I saw the way she was bound to a high-back chair with rope.

Duck tape covered her mouth. Days-old tear tracks were on her cheeks. And she was wearing a hideous homemade dress that extended to her bare feet.

"Mom!" she cried, her voice muffled by the tape. Her eyes opened wide and she struggled against the rope.

"Look what the cat brought in," Mrs. Turner said to her. "Looks like your momma figured out where you were. Too bad she has to die because of it."

Sara shook her head and tried to cry out.

"You got any last words you want to say to her?" Mrs. Turner asked me.

I burst into tears. "I love you, baby. Always remember, I love you. And I'm so proud of you. I'm sorry this had to happen to you. I shouldn't have let you out of my sight."

"You got that right," Mrs. Turner said. "I would have never let her wander around the beach at night like you did. It's dangerous out there."

I cut my eyes at her, determined to find a way to defeat her and rescue Sara.

But how? I couldn't overpower her—not with her having a gun. I had to think of something else, and think of it fast.

Mrs. Turner asked Sara, "Would you like to say a few words to your momma before I take her away?"

She nodded.

Mrs. Turner went to her, and in one swift motion ripped the duck tape from her lips. Sara cried out in pain, then shouted, "Don't you hurt my mom!"

"I'm your mother now," Mrs. Turner said. "Don't you ever forget that."

Think, think, think, I urged myself. There's got to be a way out of this.

"Mom, I'm sooo sorry I walked home by myself," Sara said, alligator tears spilling down her cheeks. "I didn't know this was going to happen. Please forgive me."

I remembered that my cell phone was in my pocket. It was my only chance.

It would be tricky, though. I'd have to reach inside my pocket and press the 'A' key long enough for it to speed dial Randy's number. Then maybe—just maybe—he'd hear what's going on and send help.

"A.J., are you going to talk to Sara, or are you going to stand there with that glazed over look on your face?" Mrs. Turner asked me.

"I...I'm just trying to collect my thoughts," I said as I nonchalantly slipped my hands into my pockets. "I want to make sure I say the right words to Sara, since this is our last farewell." My right hand found the phone. I traced a finger over it until I found the volume button. I pressed it to lower the sound so Mrs. Turner wouldn't hear Randy if he answered.

I looked at Sara, and as I felt around the keyboard for the 'A' button, I said, "Sweetheart, there's so many things I want to say to you. You've brought so much joy into my life. I know you're going to be an extraordinary woman. And please, please don't turn your back on your talent like you've been doing. You're an incredible musician, better than I could ever hope to be. Make sure you don't waste it." I pressed what I hoped was the right button. Now it was up to God and Verizon to save our lives.

"Mom, stop!" she cried. "I'm not going to let you die!" She turned her tear-streaked face to Mrs. Turner. "Please let her go! I'll do anything if you'll let her go!"

"Too late, sweetie," Mrs. Turner said. "She'll spoil everything for us if I let her go. But you'll get over it. I'll love you just as much as she does, maybe even more."

"Mrs. Turner is right," I said.

Sara shot me a surprised look. She didn't know I'd said Mrs. Turner's name aloud as a way of letting Randy know where we were in case I had successfully connected to his phone. "You'll forget all about me in time," I continued. "But Mrs. Turner will be there to take care of you."

Mrs. Turner beamed. "Well said, A.J. I'm proud of you for taking this so well."

"No! Don't kill her!" Sara pleaded. "I need my mom! Don't you understand that?" She looked at me. "Please, do something!"

"She can't," Mrs. Turner said. "I've got a gun and she don't. Looks like I win."

"I hate you!" Sara shouted. "You hear me? I hope you go to hell, you stupid old bitch!"

Mrs. Turner slapped her hard across the cheek. "You shut up, you ungrateful little slut! I take you into my home and this is the thanks I get? You're no better than those other girls! I ought to put a bullet in your skull right now, along with your momma. Then we'll see who goes to hell!"

"Stop it!" I begged. "She's only trying to protect me. She didn't mean those things." I turned my gaze to Sara. "Apologize to Mrs. Turner, honey. Tell her you're sorry."

I prayed she would have enough sense to calm down and do as I asked. At least she might live to see another day if she did. But if she didn't...

To my horror, Sara spat at Mrs. Turner. "I'll never apologize to this ugly bitch!" she snarled. "Not if she's going to hurt you!"

"Then you're both going to die!" Mrs. Turner declared. "First your mom, then you. That way, you'll have to watch me blow her brains out. That's what you get for being so disrespectful!" She jammed the gun's muzzle against my forehead. "Time to meet your maker, honey. Better say a prayer."

I closed my eyes. This was it; I was going to die right here in front of my daughter.

"What the hell's going on here?" Randy's voice boomed from behind me.

I opened my eyes in time to see a disgruntled expression spread across Mrs. Turner's face.

"Randy, boy, so glad you could join the party," she said. "Take a number. I'll get to your execution just as soon as I finish these other two."

I didn't dare turn my head; not with a gun shoved against it. But I could sense Randy drawing closer. He said, "I don't know what this is all about, but you need to put that gun down. I'm sure we can talk through this."

"A little late for that, I'm afraid," Mrs. Turner said.

"Daddy!" Sara cried out. "Please do something! She's going to kill Mom!"

"No she's not," Randy said, his voice surprisingly calm. "She's going to give me the gun and we're going to talk. Right, Mrs. Turner?"

She cocked the trigger. "I wouldn't bet your wife's pretty head on it. Now back off."

"You have to listen," Randy said. "I called the police. They'll be here any minute. Do you want to go to jail for the rest of your life?"

She laughed. "Obviously you're out of the loop, son. I don't have much of a life left. God's already handed me the death penalty. So I have nothing to lose. Besides, I think you're bluffing. Why would you call the police if you didn't know what was going on until you got here?"

"I heard it on my phone," he explained. "A.J. called me."

Shit, I thought. Not a smart thing to tell her.

"Where's your phone?" she demanded, pushing the gun harder into my skull.

"In my pocket."

She reached into it and pulled it out. "You little bitch! Think you're pretty smart, don't you? Well, I'll show you!"

"Mrs. Turner, don't!" Randy yelled.

I heard his footsteps grow closer. I wanted to cry out for him to stop, for him not to put himself in danger. But before I could speak, Mrs. Turner took the gun from my head and aimed it at him.

"Daddy, look out!" Sara screamed.

The blast from the gun was deafening. I turned and saw Randy lying on the floor, blood spilling from his chest.

"Daddy! No!" Sara shrieked.

"Dear God," I gasped. "What have you done?"

"The same thing I'm going to do to you," Mrs. Turner said. "That is, if we stop having interruptions." She put the gun back to my head. "Except yours is going to be a lot uglier." She glanced at Sara. "Hey, baby girl, you ready to see your mommy's brain splatter all over everything? It'll be just like those horror movies you teenagers like to watch. Except it's a lot gorier in real life."

"Mrs. Turner, please. I beg of you," I said.

"Don't beg. It doesn't become you, A.J."

Another gun blast rang out, this one not as close.

A blood stain flowered on Mrs. Turner's shirt. Her eyes rolled back into their sockets and she collapsed to the floor.

I was too stunned to move.

"Ms. Jenkins, are you all right?" a familiar voice asked.

All I could do was stare at Mrs. Turner's still body.

"Help my daddy!" Sara shouted. "He's been shot!"

A large hand planted itself on my shoulder. "Ms. Jenkins, it's okay. It's all over now. You and Sara are safe."

I began shaking all over. "Is she...dead?" I asked.

Chief Bowers took his hand from my shoulder and knelt beside Mrs. Turner. He felt her neck and said, "She's gone. She can't hurt you anymore."

I looked over my shoulder. Two Folly Beach officers were tending to Randy. One called for an ambulance on his walkie-talkie.

"Good thing Officer Berry is a sharp-shooter," Chief Bowers said, rising to his feet. "It was a difficult shot, but he had to take it. You owe your life to him."

"And to Randy," I said. "He took that bullet for me."

He nodded. "Then he's a brave man. Now why don't we untie your daughter?"

I snapped out of my near-comatose state and ran to her.

"You're going to be okay, baby," I said as tears of joy flooded my eyes. I wrapped my arms around her and kissed her cheeks.

"Just get me out of this freakin' chair," she said.

I helped Chief Bowers free her. When she was able to stand, she threw her arms around my waist and pressed her head into my chest. "I love you, Mom. I'm so glad you didn't get killed."

We held each other for a long while, both of us finding it hard to speak through our tears.

Finally, she asked, "How did you know I was here?"

I smiled. "I had a little help from a psychic. And a dream."

She gave me a puzzled look.

"I'll tell you all about later, sweetie."

We turned our attention to the officers hovering over Randy. "Is he going to be okay?" Sara asked me.

"Your daddy's tough," I said. "And very brave. If anyone can survive, it's him."

"He saved our lives, Mom. You should give him another chance for that."

"Please, honey, not now." I kissed her forehead. "One thing at a time, okay?"

Minutes later, the rescue squad and EMS arrived. So did Suzanne.

She ran straight to Sara.

"Oh, my God, I'm so glad you're okay!" she squealed, wrapping her in a bear hug. "What the hell happened? I heard all the sirens and rushed right over. Then I saw Randy and..." She looked down at Mrs. Turner. "Poor thing. She was such a sweet lady. Who shot her?"

"It's a long story," I said. "But trust me, she was anything but a sweet lady."

Chief Bowers approached me and said, "They're taking Randy to the hospital now. I'm afraid it appears to be pretty serious—he's lost a lot of blood."

"Do you think he'll live?" Suzanne asked.

"Only time will tell, ma'am." He looked at me and added, "If you believe in God, this would be a good time for you do some heavy duty praying for him...he's going to need it."

chapter 39

CHIEF BOWERS DROVE us to the hospital in his cruiser. Sara and I sat in the back and were mostly quiet, our thoughts focused on Randy. Suzanne sat up front and made up for our silence by rambling on and on to the chief about her plans to write a screenplay based on the events of the past few days.

"It'll be awesome," she told him. "I can get Kathy Bates to play Mrs. Turner. And you—you can play the chief. I know you don't have any acting skills, but I think you'd be a natural. All you have to do is act like your typical grumpy self. And I'll play the role of me, the visiting superstar actress." She swiveled her head around and looked at me and Sara. "You guys want to be in it? It's about time you broke into the movies, A.J. And Sara, you're sooo photogenic. The camera will love you!"

Sara and I looked at each other and rolled our eyes.

While Suzanne continued to bend Chief Bower's ear, Sara nuzzled her face into my neck and whispered, "Do you think Daddy's going to be okay?"

"Sure," I lied. "He's a strong man, honey. He'll be fine."

The truth was I didn't think he was going to make it. He'd lost a lot of blood, and I could tell by the expressions on the paramedics' faces who'd attended to him that he was in bad shape. So here I was, once again having to prepare myself for the worst. It was as if one nightmare had ended only to be replaced by another.

We crossed the bridge that spanned the Ashley River, giving us a spectacular view of the Charleston Peninsula and her proud harbor. Like an old friend, it seemed to welcome me home and whisper that I should have never left.

"Something's got to change," I murmured under my breath.

"What are you talking about, Mom?" Sara asked.

I planted a kiss on top of her head. "I was just thinking out loud, sweetie. The past few days have caused me to do a lot of soul searching, and I've realized too much of my life has been spent making albums and doing concerts. I should have spent more of that time with you—and your dad. I can't believe I got so caught up in my music. I can't believe I've been so selfish."

She shrugged. "Why don't you quit, then?"

I smiled. "That's what I was thinking. Maybe it's time to retire from the performing part of the business. I can still write songs; I love to do that. But I'll let other people sing them. And I can write them right here in Charleston. I think it would do us both good to get away from that open air asylum known as California."

Sara raised her head, eyes wide-open. "Oh-my-God, don't tell me you're actually thinking about moving here?"

I stroked her hair, oily from being unwashed. "Why not? It's a great place to live."

"Mom! You can't be serious! I heard the schools suck here. Besides, I'd be too far from Alex!" She let out a gasp. "Holy crap! I almost forgot Alex is here! Why isn't he with us? Is he at the house?"

"I'm afraid your boyfriend is a fugitive," I informed her.

She narrowed her eyes. "What's that mean?"

I sighed. "Don't they teach you anything at school? A fugitive is somebody that's running from the law."

Her forehead creased. "Running from the law? Why would Alex do that?"

"Long story. But to put it in a nutshell, we thought Alex had something to do with your disappearance, so he got scared and ran."

"*Ran?* Ran where?"

"Nobody knows. He's been in contact with his dad, but he won't tell him where he is."

She thought this over for a moment and said, "You really believed Alex had something to do with me going missing? That's so ridiculous!"

"Not really. Not when the police found blood and semen on the blanket you shared with him."

She looked stunned. "Did you say *semen?*"

I nodded. "Yep, semen. Any idea how that got there?"

"No...I mean, we kissed and stuff like that, but we didn't do anything else."

"Did he try to have sex with you?"

She let out a sigh. "Mom, he *always* tries to have sex with me. Every boyfriend I've ever had has tried to get me to have sex. It's just the way things are. But I have enough sense to say no."

I patted her knee, beaming with pride. "Good girl. It's nice to know I can trust you."

"Although you never do," she retorted, folding her arms across her chest. "So I don't get how that semen stuff got on the blanket. It doesn't make any sense."

I felt a blush coming on. "Maybe you should discuss that with Alex," I said. "His dad has a theory, but I really don't want to go there."

She gave me a quizzical look but didn't say anything.

"So can you enlighten me on how blood got on the blanket?" I asked her.

"I cut my heel on a freakin' shell," she explained. "And I still can't believe you guys thought Alex would hurt me. That's so bogus."

Chief Bowers whipped the cruiser into the parking lot of Roper Hospital. As we came to a stop, Sara looked down at her homemade dress and said, "I can't believe I'm going in there looking like this. That crazy old bitch—" She covered her mouth with her hand. "Sorry, Mom, I meant that crazy old *witch* made me wear this. She said she made it especially for me. Can I burn it after I take it off?"

"Sure," I said. "But you might want to reconsider. You're gonna need something for the prom, aren't you?"

She giggled and slapped me playfully across the shoulder.

It was a short respite from the seriousness of the situation we were about to face.

A situation that could end up haunting both of us for the rest of our lives.

chapter 40

AFTER DODGING THE dozens of reporters and paparazzi waiting for us in the parking lot, we entered the hospital through a 'special' door, where we were greeted by two security guards.

"Follow us," one of them said. "We're going to take you to a private waiting room. We'll have one of our men posted outside the door to keep reporters out. But I doubt it's necessary; the room we're taking you to is accessible only to authorized personnel."

The room was located on the top floor and was furnished with a sofa that sagged in the middle, a couple of straight-back chairs, a TV that worked intermittently, and a coffee pot that didn't work at all. But the view made up for it—a sweeping, panoramic vista of the Charleston Harbor and the Arthur Ravenel Bridge.

"It looks like two giant sailing ships," Sara said as she admired the bridge's towering twin spans.

I had to agree, with a little imagination you could visualize the sails of two giant ships as they made their way eastward, crossing the Cooper River from Charleston to Mt. Pleasant.

Although the view was captivating—especially now that night had fallen and the light from the full moon shimmered on the still waters of the harbor—it couldn't offer enough distraction to keep our minds off of Randy and the surgery he was undergoing. From what we'd been told, the bullet had entered his chest and had traveled all the way to his abdomen, leaving a path of destruction along the way. Thankfully, no major organs had been damaged, which made his prognosis favorable, as long as the bleeding could be controlled. As one hospital official put it: "Be cautiously optimistic, but also realize that things can be going along fine one minute, then the next minute..."

The official never elaborated on the 'next minute' part, but it didn't take a rocket scientist to fill in the blanks.

Finally, after waiting nearly four hours, a pudgy, balding surgeon by the name of Dr. Lewis entered and told us Randy was on his way from the operating room to intensive care.

"He did well," he told us, much to our relief. "We were able to remove the bullet and stop all the bleeding."

Sara's face lit up. "So that means my dad's going to be okay, right?"

He hesitated before answering—never a good sign when it comes to a doctor.

"The next twenty-four hours are going to be critical," he said. "There could be complications, so we're certainly not out of the woods yet. But I'd say he has a good shot at a full recovery." He shook his head and laughed. "I've got to remember not to say 'good shot' when it comes to gunshot victims. Sounds a little weird, doesn't it?"

We all smiled and chuckled at his feeble attempt at humor. Then Sara asked, "Can I go see him?"

Dr. Lewis replied, "In a little while. They want to make sure he's stable before he has any visitors. And I'm afraid only two of you will be allowed at a time. ICU regulations."

"Will he know we're there?" I asked. "Will he be conscious?"

Dr. Lewis made a rocking gesture with his hand. "He'll be in and out. But even so, go ahead and talk to him. It's a scientific fact that patients respond positively to a love one's encouragement, even if they're not fully awake." His beeper went off. He looked at it and said, "I've got another emergency coming in. It's been a busy day. But before I go..." He reached into the pocket of his scrubs and took out a folded piece of paper. "This is all I have, but I'd sure like to get your autograph, Ms. Richardson. I've always been a big fan of yours. I thought you were awesome in *Revenge of the Pharaohs*."

Suzanne took the paper from him and scribbled her name on it. When she handed it back, Dr. Lewis looked at me and said, "How about you, Ms. Jenkins? I'd sure like to have yours too. My wife is a big fan of your music."

I told him okay and wrote on the paper: *Thank you, Dr. Lewis, for saving Randy's life.* I figured it might be a good way to ensure that he took good care of Randy. After all, it would be pretty embarrassing for the doctor to show the autograph to his friends and then have to tell them that Randy died while under his care.

After he left, we busied ourselves by watching TV (when it worked), reading magazines, and gazing out the window. An hour later, a young nurse with a pixie nose came in and asked for Sara.

"Your daddy wants to see you," she said in a southern drawl. "Says he misses his little girl."

Sara leapt from the sofa, her face beaming with delight as she darted to the nurse's side.

"Can my mom come too?" she asked her.

The nurse shook her head. "I'm sorry, but your daddy said he only wants to see you. He said to make sure you come alone."

Sara gave me a questioning look, like she was seeking my permission to go.

"It's okay," I said. "Don't keep your daddy waiting."

She ran to me and gave me a kiss on the cheek, then followed the nurse out the door.

"Well, what do you make of that?" I said to Suzanne after she left. "I wonder why Randy only wants to see her?"

"Don't know," she said with a shrug. "But I guess it's a good sign he does. It must mean he's conscious."

I strolled over to the window and crossed my arms. "But why wouldn't he want to see me too? Don't you think it's a little odd that he doesn't?"

"Um, earth-to-A.J, you're his *ex*-wife, remember? You probably don't rank high on his visitors list."

I realized my lips were forming a pout. I straightened them and said, "Still, it seems like he'd want to see me. I mean, he's the one that's been saying we ought to get back together."

"He really said that? So what did you tell him?"

"Pretty much that it would be a cold day in hell before it happened."

She laughed. "And you wonder why he doesn't want to see you?"

"Well, what else was I supposed to say? There's no way I'd ever put myself through that ordeal again. He says he's changed, but I don't buy it for one second. He's always going to want to flirt with his groupies and fool around with them."

"But do you still love him?" she asked.

Her question caught me off guard, but I didn't hesitate to tell her, "Yes. I'll always love him. He was there for me during the worst days of my life. And we have a connection that I don't think I'll ever find in another man." I blew out a sigh. "But I can't take the infidelity, Suzanne. He acts like it's no big deal. Recreational sex, he calls it, like that's supposed to make me feel better. He says it's not the same thing as having an affair."

"Well, he *is* a rock star you know? It sorta goes with the territory."

"That's just a cop out," I said, feeling an all too familiar pang of betrayal well up inside me.

We talked some more until the nurse with the pixie nose returned.

"Ms. Jenkins, you need to come with me," she said. "Your husband wants to see you now."

"Ex-husband," I corrected her. "We're divorced."

Suzanne gave me a hug and told me to give Randy her love. I followed the nurse, who led me through a maze of hallways that only the hospital staff and doctors knew about.

When we reached the ICU ward, she pointed to a curtained cubicle and said, "He's inside there. I'll let you have some privacy, but I'll have to limit your visit to just a few minutes. He hasn't been doing well." She shuffled off to the nurses' station.

A sense of dread fell over me as I made my way to the curtain, afraid of what I would find on the other side.

My fear worsened when I heard Sara's sobs. I took a deep breath to steady myself and pulled back the curtain.

I couldn't believe the man lying on the bed was Randy. His skin was ashen, almost ghost-like. And so many machines were connected to him. They beeped, clicked, and whirred in a cacophony of competing rhythms.

"Mom!" Sara cried out. She got up from the stool she'd been sitting on and threw her arms around me. "Don't let him die, Mom," she said, weeping uncontrollably. "I don't want to lose my daddy!"

"Hush, hush," I said, patting her back. "He's not going to die, sweetheart. Everything's going to be okay."

I looked at Randy's face. His eyes were open but they didn't acknowledge me. They stared straight ahead, unblinking.

Sara burrowed her face in my chest. "He says he's dying, Mom. He said he could see the light, but he wanted to wait until you came before he goes to it."

"The light? Honey, I think they've got him drugged up and he's seeing things."

"No, I'm not," Randy said. His voice was weak and hoarse.

Sara and I walked to the side of the bed. "Don't try to talk," I told him. "You need to save your strength."

He reached for my hand. With our fingers intertwined, he said, "I'm glad you're here. There's so much I want to say to you before I die." His other hand reached for the cannula in his nose. "This thing is bugging me. Can I take it out?"

I moved his hand away. "Not a good idea, Randy. It's giving you oxygen. You might need it."

"I won't need it when I'm dead."

I sighed. "Randy, stop talking nonsense. You're going to be fine."

"No, I'm dying. I can see the light in the distance. That's why I want to make my peace with you."

Sara's sobs grew louder. "Don't go, Daddy. Don't go!"

A smile materialized on Randy's pale lips. "I love you, baby girl. Just like I love your mommy. I know she doesn't believe it, but she's everything to me. Always has been, always will be. I would have been nothing without her."

"Randy, stop," I said as my own tears began to fall.

"It's true, babe. I realize how stupid I was; how immature I was. I should have never cheated on you."

"Now's not the time to talk about this."

"Yes, it is. I want to tell you these things before I die." He gave my hand a squeeze. For a dying man, he had an awfully strong grip. "Maybe if I had something to look forward to I could find the will to live. Maybe if you were to give me a second chance it would give me the strength to hold on."

Something didn't seem right. I got the hunch that Randy was putting on an act. But what if I was wrong? I'd feel terrible if I didn't take him seriously and something bad happened to him. So I figured it was best to play along—at least for now.

"Randy, I think you're delusional from the anesthesia," I said. "Your surgeon thinks you're going to be fine."

He closed his eyes. "I'm fading. I can feel it. Please tell me you'll marry me again. It's the only thing that will keep me alive."

"Do it, Mom!" Sara cried. "At least give it a try! Don't let him die!"

"I…I can't. I can't be dishonest and say I'll do something that I can't do. Besides, your daddy's going to be fine. I'm sure it's just the drugs they've given him that are making him—"

An alarm sounded. Randy's hand went limp.

"Oh, my God, what's happening?" I gasped.

"Mom! He's flat-lining!" Sara shouted.

I looked at the heart monitor. It showed a straight line.

Nurses rushed in, shoving me and Sara out of the way.

"Mom, tell him you'll take him back!" Sara shouted. "Give him something to live for!"

I couldn't speak.

Sara shook my arm. "Mom! Do something! He's going to die if you don't!"

"What do you want me to do?" I asked.

"Tell him you'll take him back! I know he'll hear you! Maybe it'll work!"

A nurse called for the electric shock paddles. "And get a doctor in here, stat!" she cried.

"Mom, do something!" Sara begged.

I closed my eyes and whispered, "Randy, if you can hear me, I'll take you back. Just don't die. Whatever you do, don't die!"

The alarm stopped, replaced by a steady beep-beep-beep.

I opened my eyes. The nurses and doctor backed away from Randy. They all had strange grins on their faces.

Randy's eyelids parted. He looked straight at me and said, "Thanks for taking me back. You saved my life."

A couple of the nurses giggled.

I narrowed my eyes. "What's going on here? Was I just conned?"

Sara laughed. The nurses and Randy joined in.

"I'm afraid it was a false alarm," the nurse with the pixie nose said. "One of the electrodes fell off his chest."

I placed my hands on my hips. "Fell off, my ass. He pulled it off when I wasn't looking so it would make that alarm go off." I cut my eyes at Sara. "And you—you were in on this, weren't you?"

She shrugged. "It was Daddy's idea. Don't blame me."

The nurses excused themselves. As soon as they closed the curtain behind them I marched over to Randy's bed to give him a piece of my mind.

"How dare you!" I began. "You think scaring the living daylights out of me is funny? You think it's humorous to embarrass me by making me say those ridiculous things in front of all those people? I'll never forgive you for this, Randy! Never!"

He laughed. "Oh, A.J., lighten up. At least now I know there's a chance you might take me back." His expression turned serious. "Can't we work this thing out? Can't we try to be a family again—for Sara's sake?"

I shook my head. "No. It's time for me to move on."

"But I can change…I swear, I can. I can be faithful and be the man you want me to be. I won't let you down again…I promise."

"You made that same promise a long time ago and broke it," I said. "Why should I believe you now?"

"Because I really did come close to dying, A.J. I swear, I saw the light and all that stuff right after I got shot. And now that I've been given a second chance at life, I want to make things right with you."

I looked at Sara. She smiled and nodded.

"I can't give you an answer now," I said. "It's something I'll have to think about for a long time. And you'll have to prove to me that you've changed—*really* changed for me to even remotely consider it."

"I can do that," he said.

"But first, I have to get my own life straightened out. It's time for me to step off the merry-go-round I've been on since I was eighteen. I want to move back here, back to the beach house. I want to be a Carolina girl again."

"Oh-my-God," Sara gasped. "She's really serious about this."

I flashed her a smile. "Afraid so, sweetie. Better get used to saying 'ya'll' 'cause I'm going to make a southern belle out of you."

She covered her face with her hands. "Why didn't that crazy old woman shoot me? I'd be better off if she did."

And so began a new chapter in my life, one full of blank pages that held the promise of discovering who I really am. Mistakes would come, of that I was certain, but at least they'd be *my* mistakes. No longer would I have to answer to Randy, or my manager, or my producer. No longer would I have to please my record label. No more tours, no more interviews. Time to say goodbye to the Yellow Brick Road and find my way back home.

Would I miss the music world? Perhaps. But I could still write songs. That was my true passion. And without all the other pressures I might even get better at it. After all, Folly Beach was said to have a creative, spiritual vibration. No telling what might happen if I tuned into that—just like I had done in my childhood.

Before a hurricane named Hugo turned my world upside down.

EPILOGUE

Six Years Later
Grammy Awards
Los Angeles, California

I REACHED FOR Sara's hand. It was clammy and shaking.

"Stop being so nervous," I told her, giving it a gentle squeeze. "You're a shoe-in for this."

She leaned in close to me. "I don't think so, Mom. Have you heard the competition? They're awesome."

"But you've got the best voice," Randy chipped in. He was seated on the other side of me, looking dapper in a white tux. He gave Sara a wink and added, "Besides, you're the best looking female singer to come along since you mother. So I hope you've prepared a knockout acceptance speech."

Like me, Randy was swelling with pride for our daughter whose debut album had skyrocketed to the top of the pop charts, earning her a nomination for the Grammy's coveted 'Best New Artist' award.

I was about to whisper a few more words of encouragement in Sara's ear, when I felt a tap on my shoulder.

I swiveled my head around and found Suzanne grinning at me mischievously. Her diamond-adorned low-cut black dress had certainly drawn a lot of attention, but it was the woman seated next to her that had raised the most eyebrows.

Suzanne pointed a thumb at the woman and said, "Hey, A.J., Mom was wondering if you would like to join the AARP, now that you're retired and all."

It was great to see her with her mother. Suzanne made amends with her a few months ago, and they have been inseparable ever since. Not only that, but Suzanne hasn't touched a drop of alcohol since her mom moved in with her. Guess it goes to show the positive impact a mother can have on a child, no matter how old that child may be.

"Um, I'm only forty," I told Suzanne. "I don't think I'm old enough to join the AARP."

Her mother leaned forward so I could hear her over the band that was playing. "You should come out of retirement," she said. "We miss you and your songs. Have you considered doing one of those come-back tours?"

I shook my head. "No, ma'am, I'm too happy living life without all that pressure. It's time for me to sit back and let Sara take the stage. But I haven't stopped writing songs. I don't think I could ever stop doing that."

The band finished playing and a thunderous round of applause filled the auditorium as Alicia Keys and Bono took the stage.

"This is it," I told Sara. "This is your moment. Are you ready?"

"Mom, stop! You're way too confident. And even if they do call my name, I'm afraid I'll get so nervous that I'll puke."

"You'll be fine. Just take some deep breaths."

"No, Mom, I mean it. I've been nauseas all week."

"It's just butterflies, honey. We all get them."

A hush fell over the audience as Alicia and Bono took turns reading the list of nominees. When Bono called out Sara's name, a spotlight suspended from the ceiling swung around and shone on her. She smiled at a TV camera zooming in on her and waved. As soon as the spotlight swung away, she said, "I'm not kidding, Mom. I'm going to puke."

I gave her a dismissive wave of my hand. "You're going to be fine. Now stop getting yourself all worked up."

Bono handed Alicia an envelope. She opened it quickly, but paused dramatically before she announced, "And the winner of this year's Best New Artist is..."

We all held our breaths.

"...Sara Saunders!"

Everyone rose to their feet to give Sara a standing ovation. Alex, who'd been seated on the other side of her, wrapped his arms around her waist, lifted her off the ground, and planted a kiss on her lips.

A part of me wanted to cringe. Although they'd been married for two years I still couldn't get used to the idea of Alex being my son-in-law. But Sara loved him dearly, and as long as she was happy I was happy—sorta. Still, I think she could have done better.

Sara squeezed past me with tears streaming down her cheeks. Then she made a beeline for the stage, her black gown flowing behind her. I was afraid she might trip and fall in her haste, but she climbed the steps gracefully and accepted congratulatory hugs from Bono and Alicia.

They handed her a gramophone-shaped trophy and she stepped up to the microphone.

"I want to thank all the people who made this possible," she said, sounding out of breath. "Especially my producer, Frank Bosworth, and all the people at World Showcase Records who made my album such a success." She looked my way. "I also want to say a big thanks to my dad for encouraging me, believing in me, and helping me grow musically." She blew him a kiss. "Thanks, Daddy! And thanks for saving me and Mom's life! I love you!"

The audience stood and applauded, giving Randy a well-deserved hero's ovation. Taking that bullet for me had done wonders for his career, earning him the starring role in several action-adventure films. Now, more than ever, he had women clamoring over him, although he still swears I'm his only love. And there are times, when I'm feeling really gullible, that I almost believe him.

The audience settled back into their seats, and Sara said into the mic, "I also want to thank all my fans for supporting me and buying my album! I love all of you, you're the greatest!"

Everyone cheered.

I figured she would say something nice about me next. After all, I was the one who'd labored for six long hours to bring her into the world. Wasn't that worth a little recognition?

But she didn't say anything else. Instead, she gave Bono and Alicia a goodbye hug, blew a kiss to the audience, and started for the stage exit.

I slumped in my seat and joined the applause.

"What's wrong?" Randy asked.

"Nothing," I muttered. "Nothing at all."

"C'mon, A.J., you can't fool me. Something's eating at you. What is it?"

I shrugged. "I just thought she might thank me for teaching her how to play the guitar or something like that."

A crooked grin played across his lips. "She's nervous. She probably just forgot. Don't take it personally." He gave my hand a pat.

Sara paused when she reached the edge of the stage. To my surprise, she turned and ran back to the microphone. At the same time, a spotlight shone down on me.

"What the heck?" I whispered.

Sara smiled and said, "There's one thing I forgot to mention. I want to thank the person who's my inspiration, my mentor, my hero, and my best friend...thanks, Mom, I love you!"

I smiled and burst into tears.

Sara cleared her throat. "I didn't think I was going to win tonight, but now that I have I want to take advantage of it by telling my mom something special on national TV." Her face glowed and her eyes sparkled. "Mom, Alex and I have some news for you." She looked down at her belly and rubbed it. "We really didn't plan on this happening so soon, but you're going to be a grandma."

My mouth fell open. This couldn't be happening—she was too young to be a mother. *Way* too young.

Randy slipped his arm around me and kissed me on the cheek. "Congratulations, Grandma," he said, chuckling.

I glared at him. "You were in on this, weren't you? Sara already told you she was pregnant and you both planned this, didn't you?"

He laughed. "It was Sara's idea. She came to me and asked if I thought it would be cool for her to surprise you at the Grammys."

"And, of course, you said yes." I crossed my arms and turned my gaze to Alex. He grinned at me and gave me a thumbs up.

Suzanne tapped me on the shoulder. "Maybe you should consider joining the AARP after all, *Grandma*," she teased.

I spent the next few minutes thinking things over. How was this going to affect Sara's life? Her career? And we lived so far apart now with me in Charleston and her in California. That wasn't going to do with a baby in the cards. Sara was going to need me, just like I needed Aunt Rita to help me after she was born. So maybe I should move back to Malibu. I hadn't sold the house there yet. I could stay there for a year or so and then move back to South Carolina. That wouldn't be so bad except for...

Michael Stevens.

Who knew I would run into my old high school sweetheart at a charity event and fall in love with him all over again? A *real* doctor who had been dropping hints that he might be ready to propose. How would he react to me leaving Charleston to go to California?

I glanced at Randy. He smiled and took my hand. No one understood how we could be so close after our divorce—especially Michael. But Randy had a place in my heart that belonged to only him. That's why it hurt so much when I told him I could never be romantic with him again, much less consider re-marrying him. He'd broken a trust that I held sacred, and with all the tempting women that surrounded him now, I knew he would break it again. It was better for both of us to let him have his freedom.

"You're one hot grandma," he said, giving my hand a squeeze. "How about we sneak off to the nursing home? You can put on a pair of sexy support hose and strut around in your Depends."

"Better stop along the way and pick up some Viagra, Gramps," I shot back.

Sara slipped back into her seat. She leaned her head on my shoulder and said, "You're not mad at me, are you, Mom?"

I smiled. "No, sweetie, I'm not mad. Just shocked, that's all."

"I've got a feeling it's a girl," she said, raising her voice to be heard over the rap group that had taken the stage. "I had a dream about her. If it's true, I'm calling her Savannah Grace."

Savannah Grace. What a beautiful name. Maybe this grandma thing isn't going to be so bad after all.

I drew a deep breath and smiled, ready to face a future that promised to be anything but dull.

How would it all turn out? Your guess is as good as mine.

So if you get a chance, check back with me later.

I'll tell you all about it then.

ENJOYED *SAVING SARA?*

NOW READ THE STORY THAT BEGAN IT ALL:
A Lone Palm Stands

SET IN THE Lowcountry of South Carolina In 1989, *A Lone Palm Stands* takes you back to early years of Angela Jenkins' life, when the world as she knew it was turned upside down by Hurricane Hugo, the greatest natural disaster to strike South Carolina in recent history.

Nominated for the Amazon Breakthrough Novel of 2010, *A Lone Palm Stands* will have you laughing and crying as Angela stumbles along the path from adolescence to maturity—and finds herself coming face to face with a destiny she could have never imagined.

To purchase a signed copy of *A Lone Palm Stands*, please visit www.haolsen.com. Non-signed copies may also be purchased online at Amazon.com, Booksamillion.com and BarnesandNoble.com. A Kindle version is available at Amazon.com.